TERROR GAVE ME DESPERATE STRENGTH.

I don't know where it came from, but I managed to pull my chin up to hook over my hands.

My stretching legs brushed against another rock, too small to break the surface of the swollen river. I just got my toe against it, then found a closer rock for my left foot. I was climbing again . . . sideways.

I started to hear a pounding in my ears and saw sparkles. I needed air, like yesterday! Then, with a final kick, my head broke the surface and I sucked oxygen like a vacuum cleaner.

But I had no time to sit and rest: in water as cold as that was, high thirties or low forties, you have only a few minutes before you die of exposure . . .

Look for all of the
Swept Away
books by
Dafydd ab Hugh

Swept Away
The Mountain
The Pit*

From HarperPaperbacks
coming soon*

SWEPT AWAY:
THE
MOUNTAIN

Dafydd ab Hugh

HarperPaperbacks
A Division of HarperCollinsPublishers

This is a work of fiction. The characters, incidents, and dialogues are products of the author's imagination and are not to be construed as real. Any resemblance to actual events or persons, living or dead, is entirely coincidental.

HarperPaperbacks *A Division of* HarperCollins*Publishers*
10 East 53rd Street, New York, N.Y. 10022

Cover illustration by Bill Dodge

First printing: April 1996

Printed in the United States of America

HarperPaperbacks and colophon are trademarks of HarperCollins*Publishers*

❖ 10 9 8 7 6 5 4 3 2 1

One

I am the wound and the knife!
I am the blow and the cheek!
I am the limbs and the wheel—
The victim and the executioner!

Feeling ethereal, frightened, but determined—Charles Baudelaire whispering in my ear like a ghoul—I jogged lightly into the comforting wilderness of tree and beast, the forest that covered the shoulders of the Hag's Tooth Mountain like a shroud over an old woman.

At first, I kept hold of myself, staying quiet so I would not be heard by Dwayne Cors, my gigantic, football-hurling suitor, and especially Bill Hicks. Bill was an old . . . friend, I guess you'd say. We were almost inseparable as children, Bill and Neil Armstrong and I. No, not the astronaut; my current best friend (well, best male friend).

Then Bill just . . . vanished. They moved away

1

abruptly; and now, five years later, he reappeared on my doorstep and invited himself along on our hike. I *thought* it would be all right. It seemed like a good idea at the time.

But in five years, Bill had changed. Some sort of darkness swallowed him up, and he started hearing voices, or whatever happens to psychopaths. Lord, *he attacked me,* tried to force himself on me—right in the tree branch and palm-leaf hut that *I* built! He . . . assaulted me.

Oh hell, you know what I mean. I mean he tried to rape me.

Dwayne was outside, not too far away; but Bill was so far gone, he wasn't even afraid of a high-school football jock who looked big enough to turn pro any day now. Bill only smiled and warned me that if I involved Dwayne in our little business, Dwayne would get everything he had coming to him. Bill implied he was packing . . . packing a gun, I mean; I believed him, because I'd been packing a camping knife that I *thought* he didn't know about.

Well, Bill sure knew about it now: I'd held him at bay with the knife while I escaped outside. I slept in a tree that night, and in the morning . . . well, here I was, running into the forest, turning my back on Bill and Dwayne, and even my best friends Neil Armstrong and Samma Glynnis—trapped by the same flash flood that had trapped us, God knows where.

Or *had* Bill really changed? The more I thought about it, the more instances I remembered of him being *very* strange—even back when I knew him, when we were all kids. Maybe the darkness always lurked just below the surface of his brain, and it just needed a crisis to bring it out . . . like a flood.

Or like his girlfriend threatening to leave him. He talked about her—talked a lot about Lalla No-Last-Name (at least he wouldn't tell me her last name). Bill used the same words he had once used to describe his dog, whom I think Bill killed and dissected when he was a little kid.

I thought about that cute canine, Larceny, visualizing what Bill must have done, and I swallowed hard. Then I wondered about Lalla and couldn't swallow at all.

This boy was very, very dangerous.

And I don't mean that in the romantic-adventure sense; I mean for real. I think . . . he somehow got it fixed into his brain that *he and I* were lovers, not he and Lalla; he always said she was "just like me," and that's why he liked her. And now . . . well now, after I held a huge, sharp knife in my shaking hand, fending off a stark-naked Bill Hicks and not letting him do you-know-what, he must think that I had betrayed him—*twice*.

I was pretty sure I knew what happened to people who betrayed him.

But to hell with him—as if he weren't headed there already. And to hell with Dwayne for not being there to protect me. Who can ever protect you besides yourself, anyway? And to hell with Neil and

Samma for getting separated by the wall of water, bursting out from the ruptured Vincent Hidalgo dam! Yeah, maybe it wasn't their fault; but I wasn't in a charitable mood.

Panic gripped me, and I forgot all about not making noise. I crashed through the underbrush like a giant, rampaging bull, barely dodging trees and stumbling over fallen trunks. I panted so hard, I'm sure Bill and Dwayne heard me breathing all the way back at the twig hut; but they probably thought I was some weird kind of mythical animal: Jeanette Taylor, female Minotaur.

They must have heard something. I paused for a moment to gasp for air and heard the boys shouting far behind me. They were shouting for "Jeanette;" but I wasn't sure there *was* any Jeanette anymore. Maybe Jeanette died in that twig hut when she had to fight off the boy who once was her best friend, about whom Neil once said "it's not real until Bill sees it," and both Neil and I knew immediately what that meant.

Their voices were getting closer; they must have found the trail I left. Of course, a blind man could find the trail I left!

I backtracked my own trail, listening carefully. They stopped hollering for a few minutes; then after another couple of hundred steps, I suddenly heard Bill bellow *"Jet!"* about two or three inches to my left; well, that's what it seemed like.

They were too close; I had to freeze. I wasn't walking *exactly* on my own trail, of course; about ten feet to the side. I melted against a tree and actually saw Bill as he stomped miserably past. His skin was pale green in sunlight filtered through a roof of leaves—his lips pressed tight in silent rage. He had expected to have Jeanette Taylor to terrorize and bully for the rest of our "adventure," as Neil had called it before the flood. Now Bill had only Dwayne—and Dwayne he couldn't frighten.

He could probably kill Dwayne, and could certainly control him. (Dwayne isn't stupid, a National Merit semifinalist, but he's more average than he likes to believe.) Yet Dwayne didn't seem to have a fear mode—and fear and terror was Bill's stock in trade.

My own fear mode worked perfectly well; in fact, it was working overtime as Bill, and somewhere invisible behind a screen of trees, Dwayne, went crashing past, following the Minotaur trail that would abruptly end about three hundred yards up, where I'd doubled back.

I was surprised Bill couldn't *smell* my fear, the way an animal can. But maybe I had relaxed too soon: he paused, tilting his head to the side, listening to music that no one else could hear.

Then, Oh my God, *he looked right at me!* It took every gram of willpower I had not to duck back. I stood so still, my heart must have stopped beating. *I am the tree,* I thought, trying some creative visualization; *my skin is bark, my arms are branches, my fingers are leaves. My head is . . .*

Well, there I had me. Not too many trees have long, red hair. But I was in shadows; maybe red would become brown, dead brown lichen or mistletoe clinging to the trunk, killing the tree.

Bill turned his head, staring with the same intense scrutiny at a bole to my left. Then he looked down again, found the shredded underbrush, and continued playing Daniel Boone, tracking my impossible-to-miss, blundering trail.

It took every ounce of my courage, if you measure that in ounces, to stand still and not bolt like a rabbit as soon as they were out of eyeshot. I waited until they were out of earshot, too; then I slid gently at right angles, up the mountainside.

I didn't run and made very sure I didn't leave a trail, or not much of one. They'd need an Indian scout to track me the second time. Wrapping my arms around myself and ignoring the huge, gaping hole in my soul, I cut roughly northwest around the Hag's Tooth clockwise, not pausing even to rest until I'd gone a mile at least. There was no way I could get lost; I stood on the shoulder of the biggest mountain rising from the entire flood plane.

At last I stopped panting. When my breath and heart slowed to normal, I breathed as quietly as I could and listened to the silence.

The silence was pretty noisy. The first thing I noticed was the incessant buzzing of some insects all around me. I began to hear beats in the buzz—was that some kind of code communication? It sounded like the "hole in the sound" you get when you tune a guitar and strike two strings that aren't *quite* in tune.

I heard the mournful wail of a whippoorwill, which ought to be the state bird of California; but I also heard the burr of a hummingbird's wings, and something flitting from tree to tree—probably a sparrow.

On the ground, I heard scurrying . . . either a mouse (ick) or a large cockroach (yecch). I hoped I would never get in such a bad state that I would have to eat one of the above.

I sat quietly, listening to the symphony of the "silent" trees, too fascinated by all the new sound discoveries to be scared. A branch fell, far away; I heard it crash through other branches and finally thump against the ground. The wind wailed like a distant chorus, and I could almost make out the words. Something big galumphed past, stepping on padded feet . . . and for the first time, I felt a twinge of fear. That could be a wolf that escaped from the repopulation in Yosemite National Park; or was that Yellowstone? Or it could be a coyote (no big deal) or a feral dog (very big deal).

Feral dogs are former pets who have escaped and turned wild; they're the most dangerous animal you're likely to encounter in the forest except maybe a black bear, because feral dogs have no fear of human beings. Their interest in us is purely nutritional.

All right, Jeanette, demanded Miss Taylor, my

inner adult; *what now? Are you going to try to catch food, or were you planning on sawing off your own foot and eating it?*

I shuddered, remembering a horrific Stephen King story about a guy trapped on an island who slowly ate himself, piece by piece, to stay alive. On the whole, I decided, I'd rather eat a cockroach.

Too bad Samma's not here, I thought. Samma Glynnis, besides being my best girlfriend, is also San Glendora's greatest expert on weird, edible things. She ate a snail when we first started out on Neil's adventure, just to prove she was more of a gourmet than the French. Samma was Australian, and I guess the Outback was in her blood, even though she hailed from the Melbourne suburbs.

But I was just plain old Jeanette Taylor, and I'd never eaten anything more adventurous than octopus sushi. Well, now was the time to start.

I did the most survival-oriented action possible: I sat and thought very hard about how I would go about catching something living to eat. Going vegetarian crossed my mind; but I was in a forest, not a vegetable garden, and I didn't recognize any of the shoots around me as carrots, peas, or corn, which were the only food-plants I had ever grown. I suppose I could randomly dig up roots and eat them, but with my luck, I'd probably chow down on deadly nightshade.

I decided to look for an animal hole, then sit and watch it until its resident emerged. I wasn't quite sure what to do at that point; vague images of leaping and pouncing like a panther flitted across my mind.

I turned to parallel the mountainside and walked as slowly and quietly as I could. I found a glade in just a few minutes, and sure enough, it was full of fist-sized burrows. Of course, they could also be *snake* holes; but I'd have to take my chances.

I crouched down to watch the nearest hole, already feeling the first pangs of the breakfast I didn't have.

An hour later, I was still watching. A breeze stirred, and I jumped . . . then I realized it was blowing from the hole to me, so I was downwind; whatever was in the hole probably wasn't smelling me.

But it also wasn't stirring. I finally got impatient; what if it were a nocturnal creature? I'd have to sit here until sundown! I picked up a small handful of little, knuckle-sized pinecones, the things you step on and embed in your foot. Moving with excruciating caution, I plucked one of the cones from my palm and chucked it into the hole.

I waited a few minutes, then threw another. This time, I heard something stirring. A few seconds later, a tiny, pink-nosed face appeared at the mouth of the hole—only for an instant, then it was gone. *Hello, Mr. Cottontail; I vant to suck your blood.* . . .

After a couple of minutes, I threw another pinecone. He poked his head out again. Then I threw another. We played like this for about fifteen minutes before he finally decided his nap was over—time to come out.

The rabbit scrabbled at the loose dirt dislodged by my bombardment and hopped into view. Then he stood stock-still, trembling and rolling his eye to watch in all directions at once. One ear was pushed forward, the other pulled tight against his head.

I tensed, ready to leap at the poor, defenseless thing, when a sudden thought struck me: suppose I caught it . . . then what?

My mouth was dry; I'd heard from a friend whose mother raised rabbits that you can easily break a rabbit's neck by twisting it. Alternatively, you can take it by its hind legs and swing it like an ax at a tree; at least, this is what Neil's father, the Naval aviator, said he was taught to do with armadillos during survival training on Elgin Air Force Base; I suppose what would work on an armadillo would probably work on a rabbit as well.

Hardening my heart against such atrocities, I set myself, calculated the windage and the Earth's rotation, and power-leapt at Mr. Cottontail.

Turns out all my concerns about what to do with the captured bunny were exaggerated. I didn't get within two yards of the blamed thing. The instant I moved from cover, the rabbit spun faster than a gyroscope and disappeared into his hole without even checking the pocket watch in his weskit. *Oh my paws and whiskers, the queen will have my head!*

The queen landed on her belly in the grass and

bruised her hip on a tree root. Then she swore like a longshoreman, but the rabbit wisely remained underground.

I lay in the early morning grass, getting soaked with dew, thinking how wonderful it was not to be drenched by floods and thundershowers; for a miracle, the sky was partly cloudy, which meant partly clear.

But my stomach was still entirely empty, and at this rate I would starve to death. Behold Nimrod, the mighty hunter!

> *Under the wide and starry sky,*
> *Dig the grave and let me lie.*
> *Glad did I live and gladly die,*
> *And I laid me down with a will.*
> *This be the verse you grave for me:*
> *Here he lies where he longed to be;*
> *Home is the sailor, home from sea,*
> *And the hunter home from the hill.*

Or so wrote Robert Louis Stevenson, when he wasn't busy writing *Treasure Island*.

"Dig the grave and let me lie." No thanks; I had to figure a better way to catch that wascally wabbit. Ominous, inchoate, nightmare images of nooses and spring-traps flitted past, but I didn't stir; I knew they were ridiculous.

Maybe I could make a long spear, wait for the rabbit, and reach out and poke it to death?

A cute idea, but I doubted the lepus would let me get that close waving a pointy stick at it. I don't know much about forest creatures, but I doubt they would have survived this long if they let people sneak up on them with sharp objects.

Besides, unless it were a *really* long spear, I'd have to get extremely close—which meant walking and making noise. The experience of the last time told me I wouldn't take a single step without alerting that long-eared bunny.

If I didn't want to "dine on a diet of roach and rat," as "mehitabel the cat" sang, I'd better think of some reasonably simple scheme. Something as easy as whacking the rodent with a baseball bat, but from a distance.

At once, the obvious hit me so hard I yelped. Not a baseball bat . . . a throwing stick!

A bow and arrow would be nice; but you need to find the right wood, chop it down at midnight on Halloween, let the wood season, carve it, shape it, make the string, and string it. I read an article; there are arcane rituals involved, eye of newt and toe of frog.

But long before primitive man used bows, he found an extension to his arm that supercharged his javelins and kept him in sirloin and rump roast.

A throwing stick is just a stick of wood with a knob at one end; even *I* could make one! You hooked the knob into the back end of your dart or javelin, then threw the spear as normal . . . except when you let go of the missile, you kept hold of the other end of the throwing stick, snapping your hand forward.

The end hooked into the javelin gives it an extra boost, sending the missile faster than a speeding bullet. Well, not quite, but you get the picture.

I grinned like a jack-o-lantern; *prepare to meet your maker, Monsieur le Cottontail!*

Thinking logically, I realized the first step was to make the javelin, not the throwing stick; I'd have to find the straightest piece of wood I could find and tie my knife to one end.

Trying to visualize the throwing-stick javelins I'd seen in the Museum of Man in San Francisco, I looked for a sapling with a trunk about an inch or so in diameter; I would cut it to about two feet long, a little better than shoulder-width. Then I'd shape the throwing stick to match the javelin.

I abandoned my glade; I'm sure Mr. Bun would never come out of his burrow after what happened last time. I found a likely sapling a few feet away, but it was green and springy. I finally settled upon a hard, straight branch from an oak tree.

I broke the branch off, then began sawing away with the back, saw-toothed edge of my camping knife, cleaning up both ends.

I couldn't believe how long it took! Here I thought it was a simple task: make a pointed stick; throw stick at animal; eat animal.

The first difficulty was that the branch wasn't perfectly straight. It looked straight enough on the tree; but when I got it off and eyeballed it end-on, it bent to the left like W. C. Field's pool cue. I tried rolling it on the ground.

After long thought, I went hunting for a better branch. It was the only javelin I would have; no sense starting with inferior materials.

I spent another hour or more meandering through the woods like a loon, staring at branches with my mouth gaping open, trying to find something, well, "arrow-straight." At last I spotted the elbow of a larger branch that looked straighter than anything else I'd seen; the only problem was the branch it was attached to was as thick as my biceps!

Leaving my pack on the ground, I spit on my hands and leapt high, grabbing the errant limb. If I weren't so tall, five-foot-ten, I wouldn't have gotten anywhere near.

I hung, then struggled into a pull-up. I let myself drop, still holding the branch; it cracked alarmingly but didn't fall off.

I tried to do it again, but I couldn't get even halfway up. Girls just aren't made right for pull-ups! I had more upper-body strength than most; but even in gym class, three pull-ups were about all I could manage on my best days.

I dropped to the ground, gasping and rubbing my shoulders. I had to figure another approach.

When I could feel my arms again, I jumped up once more, gritting my teeth as I dangled painfully from my stupid proto-javelin. I pulled my body up to the branch, then hooked my long legs up and around, just like I used to do when I was champion tree-climber of my fourth-grade class. I shuddered, remembering all the times I climbed a tree, then helped Bill and Neil up alongside me; I didn't want to think of those days: the Bill I knew then was not the Bill I knew now.

Great. Now I was sitting in a tree. Now what?

Pretending the limb was the balance beam we did tricks on in Mrs. McEwan's gymnastics class, I stood gingerly, balancing carefully and trying not to look down or think about dropping eight feet to the hard ground. Reaching my hands up, I was just able to *touch* another branch directly over my head . . . not hold onto it, just brush it with my fingers . . . like I could just do to the basketball hoop at Andrew Johnson High School.

Well, it would have to do. I held my fingers tight and pushed them against the upper branch to steady myself. Then I raised my foot and stomped down on the javelin-branch, gently at first until I got the range, then harder and harder.

I was rewarded with another crack on the fourth stomp; then on the sixth, the limb splintered, dangling from the tree by a wooden thread.

That was the good news. The bad news was that it cracked not where I was stomping, but under my *other* foot—the one I was standing on!

I felt it going. Without even thinking, I squawked

and leapt up a few inches, catching hold of the upper branch and hanging like a rhesus monkey.

Ah, much better. Now I dangled *nine* feet over the ground.

Creak.

Crack.

I looked up in wonder at the limb, much thinner than the one I'd just been standing on.

Snap.

TWO

I dropped like a rock, whirling my arms like a hummingbird. I hit the ground hard, but threw myself to the side, turning a nasty fall into an almost-controlled roll. I lay on my stomach, dazed, blinking myself back to full consciousness. I could barely breathe, and my knees felt like they'd been smashed with a hammer.

Gingerly, I sat up, swaying gently while my inner-ear tried to locate up and down. Gritting my teeth against possible agony, I bent first one knee, then the other. They hurt like all- get-out, but didn't feel broken. Not that I know what a broken kneecap feels like; but I was sure if I could move them without screaming in pain, they were basically all right.

I finally staggered to my feet and stumped over to where that damned branch still hung from the tree, the cause of all the troubles in the world. I yanked on it three times before the last tendril finally let go, bowling me onto my butt again.

"After all that," I said out loud, "that stick better be worth it!"

I set up a pair of rocks as a makeshift sawhorse, held the branch steady by sitting on one end, and began sawing away with my trusty sawtooth blade. Thirty minutes later, I was still sawing; fortunately, the knife was made of hard stuff, and it didn't grow dull. I finally had my javelin shaft.

I rolled it carefully upon as flat a piece of ground as I could find; it wasn't perfectly straight, but it was pretty close, if I did say so. I could play pool with it, if I had to, if I learned how to play pool.

I tried to attach my knife, but I couldn't get it tight enough; it kept sagging. Abandoning the attempt for Plan B, I set to sharpening the narrow end, which took another half hour. My, how time flies when you're living like a wild savage in deepest, darkest California.

When I finished, I hefted the yard-long weapon. It felt pretty bloody lethal, as Samma might say. I sighted at a spot on the moist ground and unloaded. The javelin missed the mark by a couple of miles, straying over the line into the next county; but it *did* stick! A victory of sorts: all I had to do was learn some control.

Fighting down pangs of hunger—I'd felt them too often in the past five days to pay them much mind—I practiced throw after throw, learning to control the javelin. I was right about needing a throwing stick; I could make it stick in the mud, but not even in harder ground, let alone a tree trunk. It was slow, too, more Frisbee-speed than arrow-speed.

I wanted to get some proficiency with the missile itself before unloading with the assault-spear.

I finally got to the point where I could almost always hit my mark, even though the javelin only stuck one out of three or four times. Now was the time to start on the throwing stick.

This piece wasn't anywhere near as hard to make; I didn't need anything perfectly straight—all I needed was enough lever-action to get some real speed into the javelin. I had the piece finished in a mere twenty-two minutes by my watch; and within half an hour, I was Annie Oakley and Calamity Jane all rolled together. Well, you know what I mean.

> *The woods are made for the hunters of dreams,*
> *The brooks for the fishers of song;*
> *To the hunters who hunt for the gunless game*
> *The streams and the woods belong.*

Well I was certainly gunless, but I don't think that's what old Sam Foss had in mind. I wasn't heading out to snap some pictures; I had blood and fur on the brain.

I stalked through the woods like Natty Bumpo, the Deerslayer, creeping from copse to copse, whatever they were, wearing a pair of deerskin Reebok-asins. Sliding through the woods, I realized I was making hardly a sound, my feet picking their own way among dead leaves and dry twigs.

I kept to the shadows, avoiding the bright patches

where the sun splattered splotches of light onto the ground like gold-leaf paint. Then a cloud drifted between us, and the entire forest became equally gray.

This is the forest primeval. The murmuring pines and
the hemlocks . . .
(Something something something)
Stand like Druids of old.

There weren't really any "somethings" in it; I just forgot the words. I wish I knew it; I only knew one long poem by Longfellow. . . .

There are things of which I may not speak;
There are dreams that cannot die;
There are thoughts that make the strong heart weak,
And bring a pallor into the cheek,
And a mist before the eye.
And the words of that fatal song
Come over me like a chill:
"A girl's will is the wind's will,
And the thoughts of youth are long,
long thoughts."

All right, so I edited it slightly. It was my own version.

Something about stalking through a forest deserted

of two-legged beasts brought out the mystic in me. I felt at one with the trees, especially when I caught the jagged edge of a lightning-shattered stump and sliced a nice gash in my arm. My cheeks puffed out and my eyes bugged, like a combination of Dizzy Gillespie and Homer Simpson—but I swallowed my shout and didn't make a sound, except for a slight gurgle. A good thing, for just ahead I saw a sunny, grassy clearing with not one but *two* wild rabbits hopping playfully and nibbling at some foliage.

Ignoring my terrible wound—I could give myself a Purple Heart later—I ghosted forward, raising my deadly device and trying not to shake. Suddenly, I got the image of an impaled bunny, a cute little Thumper with a stake through his heart, the sort of thing you'd find in those demented splatterpunk comics my little brother Jaq is always reading.

I lost my nerve. My arm dropped, and I was sick to my stomach for a few seconds.

Then I thought about the wonderful rabbit stew my mother sometimes makes, and my nerve flooded back in a heartbeat. I started to drool.

Quickly, before I could start remembering the complete Disney roll call, I stretched my arm back and snapped it forward, flicking the throwing-stick down in one fluid move.

The javelin exploded like a rifle shot, and miracle of miracles, *it hit!*

Well . . . that was the good news.

The bad news was that it didn't hit square. I got

Thumper, all right: right through the scruff of his neck.

I never knew rabbits could scream, but boy, they've got a powerful set of lungs. It was so loud, I was afraid Bill and Dwayne would come running.

For almost a whole minute, I stood frozen, staring at the poor little thing squirming around, pinned to the ground. It tried to run away, but the hunk of wood through its neck held it tighter than any bear trap.

Then it stopped struggling and lay still, panting and bleating. Its little buddy disappeared as soon as the javelin struck home and didn't so much as poke its nose out.

Feeling like the hunter who shot Bambi's mother, I flogged myself forward. My gut tightened at the sight of the rabbit, terrified out of its mind, hyperventilating, eyes as wide as millstones. It opened its mouth and hissed at me, exposing tiny teeth that looked disturbingly sharp.

"What am I supposed to do now?" I asked nobody in particular, and nobody answered. Didn't matter; I knew what I had to do: either pull out the stick and let the poor dear go, or . . .

I knelt close, heart pounding rabbit-speed, like I'd just ran a marathon. I was shaking all over now, probably a reaction to the adrenaline that flooded my veins.

I shot a rabbit once before. I went bow-hunting with Samma, and after a couple of hours creeping through the woods, she suddenly pointed and said, "Look! Rabbits!"

Quick as a wink, before I thought about what I was doing, I turned and fired an arrow. Now, I'm a pretty dead-eye shot at archery, shooting at painted targets. Even so, I was totally, way shocked when my unaimed, snap shot actually killed a rabbit!

It was dumb luck; but it impressed the hell out of Samma, the girl from Oz, which is what she calls Australia. She looked at me with new respect for several weeks thereafter. She prepared rabbit stew, and I must admit it tasted delicious.

For some reason, when I killed that rabbit, I didn't feel anything like what I felt now. Then I was trembling a bit, but I wasn't nauseated, my palms weren't sweating, my face wasn't flushed almost as red as my hair. And I wasn't blinking away tears.

I think I know why. When I got the rabbit last time, it was quick, instantaneous. The rabbit was dead before we ran the twenty feet from where I shot to where it fell. It was a little creepy; I haven't seen that many dead animals. But it was *dead,* not alive, struggling, and suffering.

This poor guy was injured—I guess maimed is a better word—and pinned; but he wasn't dead, not by a long shot.

I reached out and touched the shaft. It barely moved as the bunny kicked, so deeply was it embedded in the ground. It passed through the nape of the creature's neck, just catching a handful of flesh. What a freak shot.

I was squatting, and suddenly the damned thing

retaliated. It kicked its feet harder than it had any right doing, small as it was, and actually knocked one of my feet out from under me.

I shrieked; I'd almost forgotten it was still alive. Losing my balance, I grabbed the nearest stationary object—the javelin. Grabbed it right near where it pierced the rabbit's neck.

That's when I discovered how flexible rabbits are. The stupid rodent turned its head all the way around and *bit* me!

It *hurt*, too. Those teeth were needles! I screamed for real this time, flinging myself backward onto my rump. Then I flushed in anger, feeling like a total girl. How dare that overgrown rat bite the hand that feeds on it!

> *He was a mighty hunter before the Lord:*
> *wherefore it is said, Even as Nimrod*
> *the mighty hunter before the Lord.*

I had to act quickly in the flush of anger. I pulled my knife from my belt, looked at the painful, bleeding holes in my wrist, and with a heart of stone, decapitated that menace to civilized society.

All right, gruesome, I know. But what did you expect? How do you think all those nice cuts of lamb and veal and strips of bacon get from the hoof to the supermarket package? I asked myself these questions to limited effect. Of course, I had always known *intellectually* that somebody had to slaughter the steaks and chops I ate; but this was the first time I ever confronted the task on such a visceral level.

Whenever I caught myself looking away or feeling disgusted, I forced myself to stare directly at what I was doing: butchering a cute little bunny—a cute little bunny I was just about to wolf down. Halfway through the skinning operation, I thought I caught something moving in the bloody mess. I jumped, yanking my hands back; but I didn't see anything and decided it was an optical illusion.

Then about five minutes later, I lifted a piece of skin and saw a long, thin tendril that twitched, then bent and *crawled across the exposed muscle.*

I stared, frozen in horror, uncomprehending. Then all at once I realized I was staring at a worm.

As soon as the penny dropped, looking down at the small body, I could see several worms crawling all through it.

I hadn't eaten a thing in nearly forty-eight hours; but by God, I sure tried as hard as I could to lose the nonexistent breakfast I hadn't eaten.

I dry-heaved painfully for a couple of minutes, tears of disgust leaking down my cheeks. Then when I finished, I steeled myself and returned to the task.

Now that I actually saw them, I remembered something Samma had said last time, when she skinned and cooked the rabbit (I refused, on the grounds that I'd done my part by killing it; she had to agree): rabbits in the wild were often worm-ridden; you had to boil the meat before you could roast it, unless you didn't mind a diet of worms, something we had studied in school in a completely different context.

Angry at myself for flinching, I grabbed one of the long strings and pulled it loose, throwing it far away into the bushes. *There,* I thought; *I hope a carrion crow comes along and mistakes you for a piece of rabbit.*

Now that I thought about them, I looked up and noticed there *were* several birds circling, a few more on tree branches, presumably waiting for the "big animal" to finish eating, so they could pick at the remains. Well, there wasn't going to be much, aside from the skin, which I had no way to cure.

I got the last of the pelt off and stared at the scrawny body. I turned it over and over, plucking off two more worms, though I'm sure there were some in the muscle I couldn't see. Hungry as I was, I was up against a terrible decision: eat it now, raw, worms and all—or wait until I figured out how to make a fire?

I rinsed the carcass and washed my hands with water from my canteen—water was plentiful, and this high up the mountain, it was free of the raw sewage from the flood. Then I wrapped the carcass up in some cool, green leaves, and fought down pangs of hunger so sharp they felt like my own knife sticking me in the gut.

I was so hungry, so terribly hungry, that the thought of waiting longer while I found something burnable, some tinder, and experimented with producing friction was almost intolerable. I reached for the leaf-wrapped, mouth-watering delectable—

And stopped. Miss Taylor was speaking again. *Are you still a human being?* she asked. *Or did you throw that away when you threw away civilization?*

I narrowed my eyelids, hand still outstretched touching the leaf-wrapped meat. Blocking out most of the visuals, I listened to the forest; I heard a far-off growl, two growls, animals fighting over dominance in the pack; I heard wings flapping above me, the carrion-eaters hoping I'd move off any moment now that (they figured) I'd finished the rabbit, which was no longer in sight; the wind howled again through the trees, and now I could hear finely distinguished differences between the low wind along the ground and the higher wind at the treetops.

I smelled my rabbit; rather than disgust me, it made me salivate, like a wolf. No, like a dog, a feral dog—for I once *had* been human, hadn't I? I once got my rabbits from Vons Supermarket. A beautiful but dull and boring boy named Dwayne Cors, now lost somewhere in this very same forest with his probable-serial-killer companion Bill, had once taken me to a fine French restaurant, and he was grossed out when I ordered escargot—snails.

And not too long ago, I was grossed out myself when Samma ate a *raw* snail, just to prove that Down Under in Oz, the men are men, and so are the women.

Miss Taylor, I thought, *I am not an animal. I'm a human being.*

Oh great; now I was quoting the *Elephant Man!*

But it was a point . . . a good one. I would force myself to wait and cook the poor, delicious dear *just because I could,* because I was a human not an animal. And that's what humans do: cook their rabbits, not eat them raw.

I picked it up and stuffed it into my pack, then shouldered the pack, grabbed my weapons of war, and humped off in search of something to burn.

I knew all about starting fires, because back when I was a Boy Scout. . . .

Yeah, right. I was never in the Brownies or Girl Scouts either; but my mom was, and I don't remember her telling me they taught *her* how to start a fire without matches, either. Maybe they do now; but back in the olden days, it was strictly sexist.

I actually had matches—three of them. Which may or may not work; they'd been soaked in the flood, but they were supposedly sealed in a plastic vial. Two had worked before, but one failed. So I probably had one working match—and I sure didn't want to use it up now.

So I did what I always do, recently anyway, when I'm stumped: I climb a tree, sit, and think.

From reading the sorts of books that only boys were supposed to read, I knew the following about starting a fire: you collect *tinder,* which is stuff that burns easily and quickly, and either strike sparks into it or create heat via friction in it. It catches fire, or starts smoldering, actually. You stick little twigs and strips of dry wood in; they catch fire from the tinder. You keep adding bigger and bigger pieces to the flames until you're sticking in whole tree trunks and small buildings—then you've got a fire.

Tinder I could find: dry moss burns pretty well, as does dry grass and leaves, if I could find them. It hadn't rained for a couple days, and I was higher up the Hag's Tooth than the floodwaters reached, so I had a good shot. But how was I supposed to get them smoldering?

Wait a minute . . . a Swiss Army knife! It has a magnifying glass—I could focus the sun's rays!

Too bad I didn't have one!

Dwayne had one back at the twig hut; but I didn't think it would be a good idea to go back and ask to borrow it, presuming I could find my way back.

In the Middle Ages or whenever, they used to strike flint against steel, or steel against flint, to make sparks, one or the other. I pulled out my camping knife and stared at the blade; it was probably steel . . . but where would I get flint? I didn't even know what it looked like. I only knew it was some kind of stone because of the *Flintstones*.

That left only fire by friction. I remembered seeing movies where people rubbed a stick between their hands, with one end of the stick inside a cup-shaped hole in a rock or a hunk of wood or something. I sighed and climbed down from the mighty oak.

Finding the stick was easy; but I couldn't find a rock with a little hole the right size anywhere. I suppose all those Aborigines must make them special, a task that was probably beyond me. But maybe I could make a hole in wood with my knife.

I had seen an old, fallen pine tree while I was scouring the woods for the perfect branch for my javelin. I worked my way back, picking up along the way anything that looked like it might work for tinder.

When I reached the tree, I planned my activity carefully: first, I set up a pyramid of stripped branches for the actual cookfire, close enough to an oak that the leaves would dissipate the smoke—I didn't want Bill and Dwayne homing in on my fire—but far enough away that I wouldn't set the mountain on fire. I cut off a thin, green sapling long enough to reach from tree to tree just over the wood pyramid: my roasting spit.

The fallen pine tree was a few steps away. I found a fairly level spot where the tree had splintered when it fell; I set to with my knife, sticking the point into the soft wood and twisting it back and forth to gouge a shallow indentation. I kept at it until my forearm ached; then I switched hands and continued, gasping and panting.

I felt really faint from lack of food; I almost nibbled at the raw meat despite my solemn pledge.

When my hole was just about wide and deep enough for the first joint of my little finger, I inserted the stick and sprinkled tinder in a little heap over the hole, then arranged my steadily escalating wood chips within easy reach.

I started working the stick, rubbing my hands back and forth against each other at a medium clip with the stick in between. It must have been working; my hands started to feel like they were on fire.

After a couple of minutes, I saw what *might* have been smoke ... I held my breath and continued destroying my palms. All right; definitely smoke. *Smokin'!*

When I got the fire big enough to light an actual brand, I hopped off the tree, shielding the flame, and ran nimbly to my stick pyramid. I tripped over a root and fell sharply; sticking out a hand to break my fall, I broke my beautiful pyramid instead, scattering the wood across the fruited plain. And I dropped my burning branch!

I screamed and scrambled for the thing, snatching it up off the ground just before it sputtered out. I blew gently, feeding it vital oxygen until it flickered back to life. I clamped it against my leg while I grabbed as many sticks as I could reach and arranged them back into a rough pile, then flung handfuls of smaller twigs into the center. I stuck my brand inside, praying to ... to somebody, I guess, and stared fixedly at the flames until they caught.

And I had, by God, a cookfire.

Three

Either I was hungrier than I'd ever been in my life, or it was a small rabbit. I polished off the whole thing. It wasn't half bad; I still had a bit of salt and Tabasco sauce left over from my last good meal, the MRE that Dwayne had given me, that his father brought back from the Army. Meals Ready to Eat! Bill and I had been starving; but even then, while Bill wolfed his down like an animal, I ate my MRE slowly, trying to feel at least semihuman.

I sat back after getting outside the rabbit . . . and abruptly realized that for the first time since the flood hit us, or even before, *I wasn't afraid*. What a strange thing to notice! Maybe it was because for the first time I realized I *could* support myself off the land itself, without having to scrounge for leftover trash, or a package of something that someone had put together for me.

My God, what a chill. This was the first meal I had ever eaten in my entire sixteen years that no other human being had to prepare for me. Even when I cooked at home, I opened packages and used pots and pans that other people made; I served on plates that we bought at Target; we used flatware from Robinsons-May.

But this time, for the first time, Jeanette Taylor did everything: I killed it with weapons I made, skinned it, cooked it over a fire that was *my* fire!

A liquid feeling of satisfied accomplishment washed through me, a warm flood. I felt peace; no wonder I was confused. I'd never felt it before; not really.

I stood, still in a state of grace, and walked into the woods, javelin in hand. In less than a minute, I saw a possum. My aim was perfect; the throwing-stick snapped, and the possum fell dead. I felt nothing but elation; I didn't even mind skinning it this time.

I roasted the possum over the cherry coals of my fire, feeling very much like the Greek goddess Artemis, the virgin huntress. I debated stripping and hunting naked like Artemis, but I wasn't quite prepared to go *that* far in my romantic mythos.

When the possum was cooked, I cut it into smaller chunks with my knife and wrapped each piece separately in cool leaves, then rolled them in a plastic trash bag and stuffed them to the bottom of my backpack. I wasn't sure how long they would last without refrigeration, even cooked; but I wasn't worried. Heck, I was a mighty huntress; I could always catch more, couldn't I?

And I could always make another fire, now that I was such an expert. I kicked dirt over it, calling it a ninety-eight-pound weakling as it sputtered out.

I decided to get my bearings; I'd look pretty lame stumbling right back into Dwayne and Bill's camp just 'cause I got turned around! I circled until I found a wide clearing where I could see the peak.

I squinted: there was something strange, something I should notice. At first I couldn't see anything; then all at once, I gasped—I saw smoke! A thin thread of pale gray smoke spiraled from the peak, or else behind it, curving to my left as the higher winds caught it.

Everything poured back. I remembered who I was, where I was—what had happened. I remembered Neil and Samma, and my guilt circuits suddenly overloaded and almost fried my brains. Bill could fall off a cliff and die, for all I cared; and Dwayne, who was such a gentleman back in San Glendora, taking me to that nice restaurant and all . . . out here in the wilderness of what once had been the Sutter Stream flood plain, he'd turned into Bill Hicks's executive officer!

But Neil and Samma were my closest friends, and *they could be dying*. They even could be already. . . . I shook my head. That was their smoke—it had to be. We were already headed toward the summit of the Hag's Tooth Mountain when the flash flood struck; it was the only logical destination now that heavy water raged all around. From the Hag's Tooth, we might spot a rescue plane, assuming they had any idea where to look for us, since Samma so cleverly got Neil to change the route. And from the Hag's Tooth, we might *signal* the plane . . . say, by lighting a signal fire and making smoke?

That was Neil's smoke, I just knew it!

And here I was, relaxing down the mountain, nibbling on roasted bunny and enjoying life, the universe and everything, as Douglas Adams liked to say.

I stared at the peak and felt honor and duty and all that Girl Scout stuff I never learned, burning in me like a fire somebody forgot to bank. Oh great, just what I need. Of all the things to have to develop, a conscience to get in the way of what Samma would call my "walkabout!"

It was late afternoon, and the tree shadows were pointing east, the way I had to go. Back about a thousand years earlier, when Neil and I were planning this "adventure," the term Neil uses for his hikes, we'd spent hours studying his U.S. Geological Survey maps of the area. We considered (and rejected) climbing the Hag's Tooth then, and I remember studying the route up; we old rock climbers do it as a matter of course.

I thought I remembered noticing that the east face was the only side of the mountain that sloped gently enough to make a climb suitable for untrained kids on a hike; all other sides were essentially sheer cliffs. I thought it was the east . . . or was it the north face?

Bill and Dwayne and I had that graphically driven home to us when we tried to scale the west face, the worst side, at night in the rain. *Hey, little girl, want to learn to fly?*

Dwayne and Bill ignored me then, two days ago, when I told them "go east, young men."

I looked again at the peak, the tip of the old crone's incisor. "All right, boys," I said, "then screw you if you won't listen!" So I'm a girl—that doesn't mean I can't read a topographic map!

Gritting my teeth and chewing on a strand of auburn hair—the sinking red sun turned it true crimson—I followed the shadows around the shoulder of the Hag's Tooth; as I got higher, the forest would thin, and I'd have to think about finding a route up. It wouldn't be a one-point climb; there were still a couple of cliffs, according to the contours, the concentric lines that show how steeply the altitude rises around an elevation.

But that was where my duty lay, if you believe in that sort of thing. I wasn't Artemis the virgin huntress; I was Jeanette, the virgin high-school junior, and at this rate likely to stay that way or die trying.

But even as I walked and jogged toward the dark purple sky, Miss Taylor kept whispering something in my mind's ear. I tuned her out; I knew what she was saying and I didn't want to hear it.

I didn't want to go back for them, the dorks. And no matter how I fooled myself about being able to handle Bill, he scared the hell out of me. There was no human being behind those eyes when he tried to rape me—not even a glimmer of the old Bill Hicks to whom I could appeal. I was alone with a wild thing; and I'd face almost anything before I went back to that.

To hell with him. To hell with them both; I was furious at Dwayne for not protecting me, even while I was stamping my foot at him for always *trying* to protect me! Yes, I know; a big, fat contradiction, wasn't it?

> *Do I contradict myself?*
> *Very well then I contradict myself,*
> *(I am large; I contain multitudes.)*

I always want to say that's Ralph Waldo Emerson, but it's actually his pal, Walt Whitman. *Leaves of Grass.* I'm afraid I only got as far as the introduction. Oh well; even I can't read *everything!*

I didn't like that "large" part, unless large means tall. I was a bit sensitive about not being the thin, svelte goddess in all the Artemis sculptures. But I'll bet she couldn't do even a single pull-up.

The shadows lengthened; the trees became shade-giants, looming in front of me and waiting to grab me with their long, sharp limbs. I slowed to a brisk walk, panting, surprised at the sudden surge of confidence I felt. I've never had that great a self-image; not like Samma! But I'd tested myself, and I had passed as well as Samma herself could have done. I "scratched for my own seed," as they say.

Maybe I wasn't such a wimp after all. At least I'd done that much.

I walked well into the night; it was impossible to lose myself—there was the mountain, looming to my left. So long as I kept it there, I would walk around it counterclockwise. I finally got tired around ten o'clock, according to my digital watch—uh oh, modern technology!—and decided to spend the night.

The ground was tantalizingly soft; but I had food with me, and I didn't want the smell to attract bears or even rats, so I decided to spend the night in a tree. There was one nearby that seemed to have a lot of branches, where I might be able to stretch out.

I discovered then that climbing a tree in the dark of night is one of those chores you're always finding in romantic novels, but which fails the reality-check. It's almost impossible, unless you already know the tree like a brother!

But I struggled up, skinning myself in a couple of places. When I reached the "landing," where all the branches split off, I straddled a couple and leaned back against the trunk, then rummaged in my pack and broke out the emergency medical kit I carried, what used to be an earthquake preparedness kit before Mother Dearest gave it to me. I got a couple of Band-Aids out and patched my knee and elbow.

Then I couldn't resist; I ate a piece of possum, surprised at how good it tasted with the last of the

Tabasco sauce, surprised that it didn't bother me to think about what I was eating.

I've never felt more contented.

That's pretty bizarro, girl, I thought; I was dozens of miles from home with no real plan for getting back, trapped by a flash flood in a forest that had suddenly become a watery wasteland, stuck up in a tree a million light-years from civilization in any form—but I was content, peaceful, satisfied.

I could stay here forever, I thought; I literally could—I could hunt animals and eat wild onions and mushrooms. I didn't have to go back, did I?

Yeah, well . . . yes I did. Is a person really a person living totally isolated? Without human contact, are we even "here" at all? I didn't know; I was no Jean-Jacques Rousseau. But I did know I couldn't imagine living the rest of my life never finishing school, never seeing Mother Dearest again, never being able to call Neil up in the middle of the night to ask him whether he thought the Whiskey Rebellion was a war of liberation or nationalism.

Oh, what the hell; it's been a hoot, but it's really starting to bug. I guess I missed it, civilization; no sense tossing ten thousand years of *civitas*-dwelling out the window . . . baby, bathwater, et cetera.

I drifted off, warning myself sternly not to try to roll over in my sleep.

The rising sun woke me, as I expected it would; I was facing east, and it took me full in the face as soon as it cleared the trees ahead of me.

I stood and stretched on the branches and jumped when I discovered tiny bite marks on the remaining possum. Evidently, I'd been visited during the night; tree-rats or mice probably walked right across me, and I was so exhausted I didn't even wake. I cut off the nibbled corner and ate the rest of the piece for breakfast. I had once piece left for lunch, and then I'd have to go to work again.

I don't think I'd ever felt so satiated in my life, like I'd just eaten the entire Thanksgiving turkey without sharing with the horde of dimly remembered relatives, including gabby Cousin Letitia and grabby Uncle Mort. I put my hands on my hips as I stood on the ground, contemplating the trek ahead, and was startled to notice I'd entirely lost the "love handles" that Neil and Samma always assured me were tiny, but which always looked enormous to me in the mirror. I could've just stepped out of a Bally's commercial! Maliciously, I tightened my belt a notch past the well-worn hole I'd always used.

I was lean and hard, like one of those female volleyball players in the Olympics—not quite as tall as Caren Kemner, maybe, but with the killer's eye for those overhead smashes . . . if I ran across a volleyball net out in the woods, I'd be ready.

Bag civilization—if I just stayed out here, I'd look like a total Bundy babe for the rest of my life!

Which might be fairly short, I realized; all it would take was one bout of the flu. People used to *die* from influenza, I remembered with a chill.

I sighed and raised my brows, then shouldered my pack, strapping the belt around my hips. I resumed my journey.

But with every step, I felt a curious weight bowing me down, like something heavy dangling from my neck. Unconsciously, I felt my throat; but I wasn't wearing any necklace or choker.

I shrugged back my pack, but that didn't help; I tightened the hip-belt until I could barely breathe— but it wasn't my backpack. Something else pulled on me.

I didn't know what it was. I tried to ignore it, but the feeling of gravity wouldn't go away. I dragged on, my head sinking longer and lower with every mile.

I was really starting to get scared. There was something drastically wrong with my cervical vertebrae! Maybe I had a pinched nerve, maybe . . .

I closed my eyes as I trod heavily across a clearing and saw words burned against my eyelids like a laser show:

> *All in a hot and copper sky,*
> *The bloody Sun, at noon,*
> *Right up above the mast did stand,*
> *No bigger than the moon.*

It was the *Rime of the Ancient Mariner,* by S. T. Coleridge; I read it last summer—it's only twenty pages long—but I didn't memorize it . . . at least, I didn't *think* I did!

I began to get a little nervous; I remembered what was coming next in the poem, and at some level I think I even understood the message. But I didn't want to. I didn't want to be reminded of a duty I had left behind, a critical element of my quest that I wanted to bag and forget.

I opened my eyes and stumbled on. The mariner was right; the damned sun did stand still, right over my head, beating down on me. If this kept up long enough—days, maybe—it would dry up the floods enough that we could hike out again.

Those of us still alive . . .

I clamped hands over my ears, trying to shut out Miss Taylor. *Don't tell me!* I refused to hear. But like Uncle Remus says, "You can't run away from yerself: thar ain't no place that far."

I stopped; I saw what *might be* my route of attack at last. Ahead of me, the trees thinned in the windward, eastern face of the Hag's Tooth; a grassy plain dotted with squat scrub-pines and barrel-shaped, midget oaks sloped steeply up the shoulder of the mountain— steep, but not a killer cliff. The slope was climbable.

I had found my entry point for the summit . . . where I would either find Neil and Samma, if that were their smoke, or disappointment if it weren't.

The very deep did rot: O Christ!
That ever this should be!

Yea, slimy things did crawl with legs
Upon the slimy sea.
About, about, in reel and rout
The death-fires danced at night;
The water, like a witch's oils,
Burnt green, and blue and white.

I traced the route up the shoulder, noting where the slope turned too steep, where I would have to double back and forth or even climb an outcropping rock.

A peculiar, black line ran across the field, right where it joined with the cliff. I couldn't make out what it was. From somewhere, I heard the musical sound of rushing water, too faint to judge size, distance, or direction.

Green grass, blue sky; and then I saw it. High up the mountain, above the line of perpetual snow, white ice flickered like flames, a line of burning oil. I stared at the ice-line; it was a wall thrown up to keep me out.

There was no way I could bull my way past it. Not alone.

And every tongue, through utter drought,
Was withered at the root;
We could not speak, no more than if
We had been choked with soot.

Suddenly, the weight bowed me to the ground. I fell to my butt, rolling over until I supported myself on all fours like an animal. Like a werewolf turning from humanity to the beast!

And I remembered *them,* the two I had left behind: I finally forced myself to look them in the face.

I looked at Dwayne Cors—and Bill Hicks.

Closing my eyes, I saw them still back where I had left them by the twig-hut that I had built. My God, I realized, they're helpless! If I left them behind and climbed the mountain, I might discover Neil and Samma . . . but I'd lose those two bozos, the serial killer and the sexist pig.

Let 'em starve! It wasn't Miss Taylor speaking; I cringed when I realized it was *me.*

But the weight around my neck still dragged on me, and I knew what it was. I'd known since yesterday. I just hadn't wanted to face it.

> *Ah! well a-day! what evil looks*
> *Had I from old and young!*
> *Instead of the cross, the Albatross*
> *About my neck was hung.*

Guilt dragged me down to the bottom of the deep, deep blue. I *left them behind,* and you just can't do that.

I couldn't leave the serial killer, serial rapist Bill Hicks to starve to death. I couldn't just abandon to amebic dysentery the overlarge, overbearing, sanctimonious Dwayne Cors, football-playing hunk who never quite noticed that I didn't share his obsession with us as a couple.

I had to have closure. I had to finish the chapter and slam the book shut, one way or another.

I'd have to go back and face them, lead them up and out, and close the relationship. Otherwise, they'd weigh on my conscience like . . . like an albatross hanging around my neck.

I closed my eyes, feeling the cool breeze sweep down from the snow and ice, bathing my face like a fine mist, soothing my fevered skin. I stood, feeling the weight rolling off my back and neck. I would go back. I'd go back into the world of men again, get those buttheads, and drag their asses to safety.

I was the captain, after all; no matter what Bill deluded himself and Dwayne into believing.

The grass, the sky, the ice—they'd still be there when we got back. And maybe the three of us could make it up past the frozen fire wall, the sheer, icy cliff that kept me off the summit like the angel with the flaming sword guarding all ways into the Garden of Eden.

I sighed with regret and straightened my shoulders. The pack wasn't all that heavy; I was strong enough. I turned back the way I'd come, sun to my back, and followed my own trail leading back to the twig-hut, Dwayne, and Bill.

*   *   *

The self-same moment I could pray;
And from my neck so free
The Albatross fell off, and sank
Like lead into the sea.

Maybe Bill really was a killer. Maybe in the end,
I'd have to face him down once and for all—not just
to get myself away, like last time, but to finally finish
the scene, however it was written.

What the hell; I wasn't the same girl he'd scared to
death last time. Maybe *he* was the one headed for a
big surprise.

Or maybe I was just kidding myself.

Four

I started back jauntily enough but pretty soon got so winded I had to stop, lean over with hands on knees, and breathe. I hadn't realized I'd been going downhill from where Dwayne and Bill and I encamped all the way to the bottom of the grassy slope—and it was an equally long way back—uphill, this time.

I slowed my pace, stopping to rest every few hundred steps. Even with the lack of food I'd had over the last few days—I was sure I hadn't gotten enough vitamins; no leafy, green vegetables—I still felt stronger than when I started the adventure about a thousand years earlier. I'd toughened up.

I found a combination pace, trotting for a while, then slowing to a walk, that gobbled up the miles. I made it all the way back to approximately the right spot just as the sun set.

Now what? There was no way to tell *exactly* where I'd been; there were no signposts. I climbed

47

the tallest tree I could find and scanned for smoke, but saw nothing. Of course not! How would those two make a fire?

The wind howled like a dog that had lost its mate; up in the tree, I listened to the wind. I closed my eyes, fighting back senseless tears. I couldn't help it; a mournful wind always affected me like that.

I heard another faint sound on the breeze. It wasn't quite loud enough for me to identify . . . but it was weird, a kind of rhythmic chanting. It sounded creepy, like a tribe of antediluvian monks worshipping some elder god with thoroughly revolting sacrificial rites. Jesus, what a morbid imagination I had!

The wind died, and the sound stopped. Making the brilliant deduction, I decided to follow the wind to find the noise. I shimmied down the tree, faced roughly southwest (the quarter the wind had come from), and slowly advanced.

Whenever I got a breeze in my face, I stopped and listened; after a few minutes, I heard the chanting again, a fraction louder.

I hooked my throwing-stick into the back of my javelin and held them both at the ready position; I was taking no chances with this freaky noise!

I moved about three hundred yards, tacking left and right as the sound appeared to shift. More likely, the wind was simply confusing me. The next time I heard the noise, it suddenly clicked: it was Dwayne Cors—singing again.

I laughed silently, shaking my head. The first time Bill and I spotted him after the flood separated us all, he was singing Janet Jackson; this time it was the artist formerly known as Prince, and currently known as ink-splotch. *Little Red Corvette,* to be precise.

By the time I got close enough to make out the words, Dwayne had segued into Springsteen, *Blinded By the Light*—a very idiosyncratic version. I arrived at the very clearing I had left just in time to hear Dwayne belt out "Blinded by delight . . . wrapped up in a douche, she went running in the night," which isn't at all the way *I* remember the lyrics. Ick!

He had also invented a new key all his own. Bill Hicks sat a hundred yards away on the ground with his hands over his ears; I didn't blame him.

Dwayne Cors sat on a log—a new addition—in front of the very same twig-palace I had built days earlier. He didn't look happy; I'd have bet he was singing to try to cheer himself up, because he looked like his favorite TV show was canceled.

For some reason, I was reluctant to step out and reveal myself. I stared at the two of them utterly shocked to see them looking dirty, emaciated, completely defeated. *My God,* I thought; *they're dying! They're actually starving to death!*

I couldn't just pop out as I was. I'd be sucked into their hopeless misery. I had to bring some sort of offering, something to totally snap them out of their despair; and I knew just the thing, the perfect gift for the flood victim who has nothing: food.

I slid back into the forest, making not a single noise. Then I turned and stalked directly toward the mountain peak, heading slightly, then steeply uphill, looking for a clearing with holes.

I found one, coaxed a rabbit out by tossing stones in, and shot the poor creature without a pang of conscience; it was eat or be eaten!

When I returned to Twig-Hut Meadow, it was pitch dark. Dwayne had stopped his horrible racket, whose only benefit was undoubtedly that it kept bears away. He and Bill both sat on the log now, saying nothing, just staring into the black forest beyond the pale.

For a couple of minutes, I just watched them. Then I took a deep breath and stepped into view.

The effect was nothing short of remarkable; they like totally freaked.

Bill saw me first. His mouth dropped open, then lower and lower, and he froze on the log-bench. I couldn't see his skin color in the moonlight, but I'd be willing to bet my brother Jaq's comic book collection that Bill blanched; too bad, I've always wanted to see someone do that!

Dwayne didn't see me at first, and of course Bill wasn't giving out any clues, just staring like Monkey Boy. But after a few seconds, Dwayne's eyes caught the movement and looked at me without interest.

It took a few seconds. Then he leapt to his feet with an inarticulate, strangled cry. He pointed his finger and said, near as I can transliterate, "hunh hunh hunh" in an excited voice.

I stood still, weapon resting in the crook of my left elbow, waiting for reason to settle back into their "teched" brains. Honestly, men! You'd think they were looking at the Bounding Bogle of Arlagh Moor, or whatever that ghost was that Samma told us all about on the first night of our adventure.

The boys looked thinner, too; but their thinness was not tight or healthy. They looked like they hadn't eaten a thing since I left.

They hadn't. Bill eyeballed the rabbit dangling from my belt and said, in a weak, reedy voice, "You, ah, don't plan to eat that whole thing by yourself, do you? Can we, ah, share it with you?"

My lips twitched, almost smiling in spite of my newfound resolution not to give them anymore than they deserved. I'd never heard Bill Hicks so supplicating. He wasn't on his knees—but I knew in an instant that if I demanded it, he would do it. Anything to get himself outside that hunk of bunny.

Knowing I had that power scared the bejesus out of me. I'd never thought of myself as the slave-owning sort; I figured that went out of fashion about 1865. But just the *feeling* of power made me dizzy. I realized to my shame that I kind of enjoyed it—seeing them eye my kill and tremble like low dogs in the dog pack.

I plucked the rabbit off my belt and threw it to Dwayne, who made like a football player and caught the reception. He sank to his knees, shaking in eagerness and hunger, and burrowed into his pack for his Swiss Army knife. He started hacking at a leg.

I moved in quickly. No matter what the one had done and the other allowed to happen, I still refused to allow anyone under my protection to sink to the disgusting level of chowing down on raw rabbit. Not in my presence!

"Stop that, Dwayne! The two of you, just simmer down. Let's get a fire started; we're going to roast this thing. You two can split it; I don't want any."

Dwayne stared at me with huge, puppy eyes and nodded, bobbing his head up and down like a pigeon. It was freak-city: a few days ago, less than a week, he'd been the totally arrogant, smug, superior Giant Dude on Campus. And now, just a few meals short, he was willing to trade independence, dignity, and even his freedom for a few mouthfuls of food. The thought gave me eight-legged creeps running up and down my spine.

"No country is ever more than three meals away from a revolution," said novelist Larry Niven, and I guess he knew what he was talking about. If most people were like Dwayne and Bill, you take away their food and their toys and they grow fur and run around on all fours, barking like dogs.

I spent a half-hour showing the boys how to light a fire without using matches. I don't think they paid much attention; they were too busy staring at the rabbit, watching it in case it sprang back to life and hopped away.

I kept waiting for either one of them to say something, anything; ghost stories, blow-by-blow accounts of old football games…Even Bill Hick's disturbing predictions of a total collapse of civilization, *The End of the World As We Know It,* or whatever that song is, would have been better than cringing silence!

But the only person to start conversation was me, and I ran out of polite icebreakers after the first fifteen minutes. It's rough carrying on a conversation with guys who say nothing but variations on "you're right, Jeannie" or "that's a good point, Jeanette."

I gave up finally and just waited until they had gulped down a half a rabbit apiece, not enough to fill them up, but enough to take the edge off. I'd scare up some more game in the morning; in the meantime, we'd keep the fire burning all night, so we'd still have embers to rekindle at breakfasttime.

After eating, they tried to listen to me recount my adventures with making the throwing-stick; but they looked about as lively as Keith Richards, so I shut up and let them collapse in exhaustion.

I couldn't sleep. I lay near the fire, feeling its warmth, thinking to myself, *I've got a possible killer and definite rapist on my left, and an insensitive jerk on my right; how long until they try to regain control over me?*

I dozed; it was the best I could do. Every hour or so, I woke up long enough to put more wood on the flames, then drifted into another fitful, half-dreaming,

half-waking world where the most demented night-
mares lurked.

I fell truly asleep at last a couple of hours before
dawn. When the sun rose, shining through my eyelids, I woke. Bill sat cross-legged nearby, staring
down at me with utter contempt and loathing, a con-
torted mask of pure hatred. The boy wanted to rip
my lungs out.

But when I opened my eyes and caught him staring at me, he dropped his gaze and pursed his lips,
like he was trying to come up with the most excellent scheme for revenge. I didn't like that Bill Hicks;
of course, it was better than the Bill who felt perfectly free to strip naked and tell me how we were
already lovers in his sicko fantasies.

Even my twig-castle had fallen, and neither of the
boys seemed to be able to fix it. They just left it the
way it fell, so dependent on all the trappings of civilization that they were helpless once their junk food
and MREs ran out.

I rose, trucked into the woods, and answered
Mother Nature's call. I used a handful of ivy leaves—
there's no poison ivy in California, thank God—then
returned to Purgatory with my two bozos.

When I returned, Dwayne was up as well. He
looked completely shell shocked . . . I had no idea
whether he was having a hard time coping, or
whether that's the way he always looked in the
morning. His blond hair stood straight up like it was
gel-spiked, and he rapidly blinked his eyes. He

scratched himself through his flannel shirt, giving me a nice view of his chest.

I caught Bill staring at Dwayne too, again with that loathing I'd seen when he was looking at me earlier. That boy would bear watching; if he really was what I thought he might be, then we were already on his list of upcoming victims.

Strangely, I wasn't as scared as I thought I'd be. I knew we were going to have a confrontation; but when? I thought of warning Dwayne, but he wouldn't believe me anyway. That sort of thing just doesn't happen in the world Dwayne grew up in. I wouldn't have given it a second's thought myself except *I knew Bill Hicks.* Even as a kid, there were parts of him that nobody ever saw, places where he could have hidden Ted Bundy or Charles Manson inside his head.

"Lay out the gear, boys," I said, as much to get my mind off morbid subjects as anything. "Inventory."

We had no food; they'd eaten all the rabbit, and I had the last of my possum the day before. But water was cool; there was a small stream not too far away, and water running down the mountain toward the flood plain was all right for drinking. We had the rope, not really suitable for climbing but the best we had; three tent pegs; some cooking gear; my knife, which I wore openly now—Bill already knew about it; first-aid kit; three matches; a sleeping-bag cover (but no sleeping bag); a propane cylinder, in case we found a propane stove up in the mountains somewhere; plastic trash bags; and Dwayne had a flash-light.

The rest of the gear was just clothing—when Neil had irritatingly repacked our packs to evenly distribute the load, he'd left all the personal stuff alone, of course.

I supervised the load-up, making sure I got the rope and the tent pegs, the things that could be used as weapons. There was no question anymore about who was in charge, or who was "the captain," as Bill liked to pretend. Dwayne, who had been my first officer, then Bill's, was back to being mine, and he seemed perfectly happy. He wasn't dumb—National Merit semifinalist—but he didn't want the responsibility of giving orders. Dwayne wanted to be told what to do.

I stared at the fallen twig-palace. It was a shame to leave it, after all the work I did; but how could we carry a bundle of saplings along with us while we hiked through the woods? It just wasn't practical, and if I'm anything in an emergency, it's practical.

I did take the log I'd used to start the fire at the camp; it was smaller than the first one I used back in the woods, and I shoved it in Dwayne's pack. I threw in some kindling, too. I didn't know whether Samma had rescued any of her "supermatches," the things that looked like long, thick pieces of beef jerky that could light anything on fire.

"Head 'em up and move 'em out," I decreed, pointing eastward, back toward my grassy slope, several miles distant. As we started, Dwayne broke out into the *Rawhide* song, and I joined him. I'd watched the show on Nick, mostly to see a teenaged Clint Eastwood. Bill kept his mouth shut, staring at the ground as if worried about a trap door.

We walked for quite a while, and Dwayne finally ran out of television songs. When he finished *Rawhide,* he serenaded us with *Gilligan's Island,* the *Brady Bunch*, the *Addam's Family* (he knew *all* the lyrics, even the mysterious third verse), and the *Patty Duke Show*—I guess he spent a lot of time watching *Nick at Nite.* But he wound down at last.

I tried to contribute, reciting *The Walrus and the Carpenter,* by Lewis Carroll; but everyone just stared at me, so I trailed off into silence. Philistines!

We walked in silence, like the night. How does that go?

> *She walks in beauty, like the night*
> *Of cloudless climes and starry skies;*
> *And all that's best of dark and bright*
> *Meet in her aspect and her eyes . . .*

It wasn't a comforting image; Lord Byron decided to join a silly quest and was wounded, taken back to his rooms, and was bled to death by barber surgeons. In fact, I wished I hadn't thought of him.

But his buddy Shelley's death was even worse: he drowned!

Thank you for sharing, I told myself and my weird, trick memory.

It was almost dark as night under the trees, a thick panoply of branches weaving together over our heads and blocking out the sun . . . but the sky was hardly "cloudless." In fact, it was getting overcast again. Too bad I didn't just continue up the mountain the day before; it was beautiful then.

The light brightened and dimmed so rapidly, my eyes had no time to adjust to the change. I was blinded. At least, that's the story I'm sticking by to explain how I happened to walk right into the side of a bear.

I'm not sure which of us was the more startled, me or the bear; but I sure as heck knew which was the more scared.

That bear didn't look scared at all!

Five

The bear scrambled to its feet faster than my little brother Jaq when I caught him peeping through Mom and Dad's bedroom door. At first, I thought it was a grizzly, but that was just hysteria: it was just a black bear, I realized an instant later.

JUST! The thing still stood taller than Dwayne when it got on its hind legs, which it did while I was still back-pedaling. It growled and roared and kind of staggered forward, unsteady on its legs but not about to fall over yet.

I backed up so fast I ran into Dwayne, who hadn't seen the bear yet; his eyes were still adjusting. Bill reacted quicker, turning and running back about fifteen yards; then his conscience got the better of him, which was quite a surprise, and he turned back.

When Dwayne finally saw the ursine guest, he froze, just as he had when the wall of water first struck us. Since I was already backed up against him, I couldn't go any farther . . . it was like having my back against a mountain!

"Easy, Fido . . . nice boy—or girl, whatever. We don't want to hurt you." I tried soothing tones while pushing Dwayne gently but firmly backward. I wanted to shove him out of the way and run like a thief, but I figured sudden moves were definitely out this season.

But the bear wasn't interested in all of us going our own ways. I think he was hungry; the flood might have killed off the fish or shrunk his territory so that he couldn't find enough food. He looked at me, and I felt like one of those cartoons where the people are stranded on a desert island, and they keep seeing each other turn into lamb chops and huge, roasted turkeys.

My hands and feet started to tingle . . . I guess I was going into shock, I was so scared—because I suddenly realized the bear was about to maul me.

I'd never been mauled before; I was never a maul-rat. And I wasn't really interested in the experience, thank you. But what could I do? If I turned to run, he'd drag me down in a heartbeat!

Dwayne was no help; all he could do was throw himself in between us, which would delay the bear all of three seconds while he broke Dwayne's back, then continued after me.

The bear dropped back to all fours and galumphed forward. I surged back against the Dwayne-machine and actually kickstarted him! He jumped back, torn between wanting to save me, the woman he'd convinced himself he was in love with, and wanting to get the heck out of Dodge himself.

We compromised: Dwayne retreated far enough to trip himself, while I stumbled over him, falling to one knee. We were a matched set.

The bear rose again and charged.

Without even thinking, I raised my javelin like a pike and planted the butt into the ground. I don't know what I was thinking, or even *if* I was thinking! But I got the point up just in time . . . the bear lunged at me and impaled himself on the javelin point.

He struggled to free himself and attack me at the same time; but he was stuck at one end of the spear, and I was at the other.

The bear pawed at its injury, then shook himself violently back and forth. I hung on grimly, sure of only one thing: so long as we had three feet of wood between us, he couldn't hurt me.

All of a sudden, strong arms reached around me, and giant hands grabbed the javelin just below my own hands. Despite my earlier feelings, I suddenly felt safe and protected by Dwayne Cors . . . and at that point, I'd take all the comfort I could get!

We held tight while the bear thrashed around, trying to rip loose the sharp stick, hand-carved by *moi*. But after a few minutes, the convulsions quieted, and the bear made only halfhearted attempts to struggle free.

I clung to the javelin, and Dwayne kept his arms around me until long after the bear had ceased moving.

I dropped to my rump, dazed, staring stupidly at the carcass. *I'd killed a bear, for heaven's sake!* I felt like Daniel Boone!

I had a second or so of jubilation, then I started to get the shakes. I covered it up, and I got up and walked around and around the animal, as if I had to study the kill and make sure I'd done it legally. I was all, "Uh huh . . . yes . . . hm . . ." It must've worked, but probably mostly because Bill and Dwayne were themselves so shaky they didn't notice that I looked like I was standing in an earthquake zone. After several minutes, I was cool again, the mighty Nimrod. "All right, lay it out. Let's start cleaning it."

Dwayne turned to me, puzzled. "L—Lay it out?"

"Lay it on its side, so we can skin it and cut the meat off."

Dwayne's eyes widened and his face got a shade paler. "You mean you want me to *touch it?*"

Bill snorted, turning his withering sneer on Dwayne. "Oooh, the great he-man is afraid to touch a *dead* bear! What, you afraid its ghost is going to haunt you? You're such a pussy."

Dwayne was still so shaken he didn't even threaten to pound Bill into the dirt to prove his virility. "No, I just . . . I mean, I never thought about . . . "

"You ate the rabbit I got for you," I said. "Just think of this as a very big rabbit."

"But I was starving then! I'm . . . not even hungry

now." Dwayne's face turned beet-red when he said the last, so I knew he was lying. He's not a good liar, not like Bill. The only way I could tell when Bill was lying was his Huckleberry Finn-smile, disarming and charming. That meant you'd better put your hands over your ears, because he was about to talk you out of your last dime, or worse.

Dwayne *was* hungry; he just wasn't so hungry he could forget his squeamishness. And I had to admit, even being the one who killed the bear, it made me a little queasy to think about skinning it.

But this was survival; like I said, eat or be eaten. I was half sure that if I hadn't been the "Captain," I'd be standing behind Dwayne, voting not to touch the dead animal.

But I *was* the leader; I guess every lifeboat needs one leader. And their welfare was my responsibility. It was why I'd gone back for them in the first place . . . somehow, it had become my duty to get these doofoids up to the top of the Hag's Tooth, where we might find Neil and Samma . . . and where a rescue plane might spot us.

So I gritted my teeth, drew my knife, and (ick) did it. It was a lot harder than the rabbits and the possum; I wasn't surprised, since the thing weighed five times my weight! At first, I had to keep pushing Dwayne over to the bear, pushing him down, making him help us roll it over. But after a while, he was moving under his own impulse power, though he was still pale green.

Bill, of course, had no squeamishness at all; and that made me even more uneasy. His knowledge of anatomy was excellent—and it seemed to come from personal experience, not just from book-reading. I doubt he'd ever skinned a bear before; he said he hadn't. But I was pretty sure he'd skinned and dissected a lot more animals than what you usually get in biology class.

In fact, from the way he stared hungrily at me when he thought I wasn't looking at him, I got the creepy feeling that he had a lot of firsthand, personal experience with *human* anatomy, too. Not from a book.

I figured we were about three hours from the slope where we could climb, and it was only eleven o'clock in the morning. We'd have plenty of time to make it there and even climb to the top before it got fully dark, which it did these daylight-savings days after eight P.M.

We had time to build a fire and cook the bear meat; and I decided it was a good idea to do it. After all, it's entirely possible that Neil and Samma had *no* food up there . . . if they were even up there at all. Cooked meat lasts much longer without refrigeration than raw meat.

"Um, Jeannie?" asked Dwayne.

"It's Jeanette, Dwayne; don't call me Jeannie!"

"Sorry. Can I start the fire? I always wanted to learn how to do that."

Bill sighed with exasperation, rolled his eyes,

shook his head—he was so much like the old Bill I'd
known as a kid, that once again I started to doubt
that he'd really done what I remembered him doing.
Maybe he wasn't really trying to violate me—maybe
I just misunderstood everything—maybe it's just me,
I'm the spaz. . . .

No! I forced myself to stop thinking that crap. I
had to hang onto what I *knew,* what Bill was. If I
didn't, he'd suck me in again, and I'd wind up dead as
dirt, either before or after he had his way with me.

I shut off the flood of good memories of Neil and
Bill and me when we were all kids; this wasn't the
same guy; I had to keep telling myself that until I
really believed it.

My life depended on it.

I showed Dwayne how to put the kindling
around the hole, then poke a stick in and rub it to
make friction. He started doing it and actually got
a thin stream of smoke in just a few minutes . . .
much faster than I was able to do it, even after I'd
done it twice. I was really annoyed; I don't know
why. It was a pretty practical skill to have, and if
I'm anything in an emergency situation, I'm—
Well, I guess I'm not quite as secure as I thought I
was.

We spent a couple of hours roasting bear meat.
Bill was pretty excited . . . scary, in fact. He kept licking his lips, like he couldn't wait and wished we
weren't around, so he could eat it raw. He insisted we
roast the heart; Dwayne turned green and staggered

away, saying he was still sick from the amebic dysentery he'd had for several days after drinking contaminated water.

I almost followed him. Then I remembered that I'd seen beef heart at the supermarket. (Near the meat section where you could buy severed lamb heads—with the *teeth* still in them!) It was kind of dorky to spaz out over a bear heart when half the world ate beef heart; well, maybe not half, but lots.

I acted totally cool, like it was the most natural thing in the world to watch someone cut open the chest of a black bear and rummage around looking for particular innards. "I think I've got something here," mumbled Bill; then he shook his head. "Nah, this is the liver. Hey, maybe we should eat that, too? Liver's good for you."

"Not bear liver," I said automatically, forcing myself to watch him. I kept looking away, but I didn't want him to think I was weak. It was a fragile balance; anything could tip it over. I wanted Bill to stay under my control.

"What's wrong with bear liver?"

"It's poisonous."

"Why would it be any more poisonous than chicken or beef liver?"

I sighed. "I don't *know* why it's poisonous; I just know I probably definitely heard it on the Discovery Channel: bear liver is deadly. Go ahead and eat it if you want; we'll bury you deep."

Bill glared at me, pushing his tongue first in one

cheek, then the other, trying to decide if I were serious or not. "You're not just BS'ing me?"

"Bill, trust me. I'd love nothing more than to eat out the entire abdominal cavity of this thing. But the liver is deadly poison, and if the javelin punctured it, it's probably contaminated everything around there. Besides, I'm sure we perforated the intestines, which means the inside of the bear is full of you-know-what, anyway."

"I found a heart."

"Congratulations, Tin Man. Now maybe if I just click my heels together three times and say 'there's no place like home,' I'll wake up."

"I think I can wash it off, and we can roast it. Jesus, it's big!" He held up a bloody, disgusting glob of something, presumably the organ in question.

"Yummy."

"You going to join me in this?"

"Is there room for both of us in there?"

"Or am I going to have to eat it all myself? If you don't have the stomach for it, I'll—"

"Oh, I'll have some. But you'd better rinse it off really clean. We'll cut it in thirds; we could all use some bear-courage."

It took some doing to drag Dwayne back and make him eat a couple bites of the heart. He was not a happy camper. "Didn't you ever eat beef heart?" I asked.

He shook his head in horror.

"Squid? Escargot—Oh, I forgot." I'd ordered

snails in the French restaurant he took me to, Le Petit Homard, a.k.a. The Little Lobster. It totally grossed him out.

"Tripe?" suggested Bill maliciously; tripe was cow intestine.

Dwayne had passed beyond nauseated to truly ill, but I couldn't resist. "Sea cucumber?"

He stood and began walking rapidly around the fire, breathing deeply. Evidently, the mighty Olympian athlete had a stomach that was a total pushover.

The bear meat was good, especially since I was hungry. It was chewy and had a lot of fat. Ordinarily, I like to eat a low-fat diet; but in a survival situation, fat was the *best* thing to eat, since it has nine calories per gram . . . a much higher calorie-count than muscle meat. I wasn't worried about putting on weight.

The taste was sharper than cow, which I guess is what people mean when they say something is "gamey." We cooked it to death, well done, just to kill any parasites that infested the thing; I remembered the rabbit with the worms burrowing through its flesh.

We had a quarter-ton of meat, almost literally. Naturally, we only roasted a few pounds, since that was all we could carry. We left the rest behind when we continued our trip; I was sure it wouldn't lie there for long.

Finally, we reached my entry point for the climb, Jeanette's Meadow, I called it. "Come on, boys; let's get closer and scout the route."

We walked toward the cliff, and the strange,

unidentified black line I'd seen the last time I was there grew sharper. I started to feel a vague sense of unease . . . the line was not good news, I knew, but I didn't know why.

I found out another couple of hundred yards up the hill. We walked across spongy, marshy ground, wet but high enough up that it wasn't a swamp, like the valley floor. We walked through wet grass, and in a couple of minutes my pants were soaked as thoroughly as if I'd waded through a mountain stream.

Everywhere, I smelled cloying honeysuckle, anise (which smells like licorice), and the faint hint of mint. Then I brought my eyes down from the cliffs to look at the black line, and my heart sank: it was a ridge. The slope did *not* lead right up to the mountain, as I'd hoped; it was an unconnected rise, and we had to climb down into another valley.

The sound of rushing water got louder and louder, and I realized even before we crested the ridge that we had to cross a gorge cut by a rushing river, a river probably swollen with snow runoff from the Hag's Tooth and buckets of rain.

Sure enough, when we got to the bunny-slope summit, I looked straight down forty feet or so into a torrent that made the last one we'd crossed, days ago, look like an offshoot stream. Who knows? Maybe it was!

We'd almost lost Dwayne on the last crossing. I decided there and then that we would *not* lose anyone this time.

"Okay, men . . . any suggestions?" I turned to Dwayne, and he was chewing his lip—probably remembering the last time, as well. But when I turned to Bill, I realized instantly that my guess last time was on the money: Bill Hicks had a phobia about drowning; he was terrified of rushing water.

He didn't say anything; he didn't need to. His skin was so pale, it looked like printer paper, and he was already hyperventilating even just *looking* at the torrent. Well, there was no way around it; the river continued off in both directions as far as I could see, which was a considerable distance from atop the ridge.

I felt bad for Bill, but I couldn't bring myself to touch him; so instead, I put my hand on Dwayne's shoulder, hoping neither he nor Bill would get the wrong impression. "Okay, guys," I said, trying to sound gruff, like I imagine an Army sergeant sounds, "let's get closer and eyeball it."

Nobody seemed to want to move, so I stepped forward first and carefully started down the steep slope toward the river.

Carefully, hah! I started walking, but each step down was like two or three feet into soft, wet earth. After a while, I lost my balance and had to start bounding to avoid falling; I felt like the Bounding Bogle of Arlagh Moor. Then I was careening pell-mell down the cliff, and it was a short, off-balance step from there to sliding on my rump.

I slid for twenty feet, screaming and windmilling

my arms; then the ground leveled, and I was sliding horizontally . . . straight for the river!

I flashed past a tree, and instinctively I lunged. I overshot, the tree smacking me hard as a kicking mule in my right breast and armpit; but I wrapped my arms around it anyway and jerked myself to a stop, my feet actually dangling over the sheer river bank.

I lay like that for a few seconds, trying to suck oxygen inside; the tree had knocked the wind out of my sails. When I felt a little more in control, I stood shakily and looked up the slope at Bill and Dwayne, who were staring in amazement, like watching an acrobat at the Cirque du Soleil.

"Well?" I demanded, as loudly as I could with no breath. "You coming, or what?"

Six

ill and Dwayne tentatively started down the slope, figuring they would just go slower than me and avoid the rush. Bill was in the lead, and he started speeding up for the same reason I did . . . that old devil, gravity. Within a couple seconds, he was slipping and whooping, flapping his arms like a giant bird. Then he was down on his back, sliding down the slick, muddy slope.

Dwayne was next, and I eagerly watched to see that oh-so-superior athlete drop like an oaf . . . and would you believe it? He stayed on his feet all the way down! He wasn't even off-balance; he hit the marshy bottom at an easy trot, gently braking to a stop and looking blankly at us. He probably stifled a yawn when I wasn't looking.

The floor of the gorge was a swamp. The floodwaters weren't dropping; if anything, in this cut they were still rising. The river was enormously swollen—if it were normally this size, it would definitely have been marked as a major, navigable water-way on the USGS map. I didn't remember seeing it at all, which means it grew from a trickle to the Missis-sippi in just a few days—probably the combination of runoff and the flood itself.

It wasn't that it was particularly wide; it was maybe fifty feet, ten feet more than the last one we'd crossed. The difference was the sheer volume and velocity of the water. The other river had a current, but I could wade through it, even waist high, just by hanging onto the rope above my head.

There was no way I could shove my way through this torrent! There was only one chance, and it seemed pretty bogus: somehow, we had to get the rope across first, then we'd dangle from it upside down and climb across *above* the river.

The wash flowed from right to left, facing the Hag's Tooth; so it probably was the headstream from which the last river was just a branch, feeding into the lagoon we fell into—or the *billabong,* in honor of Samma, the girl from Oz.

I explained my idea to the boys. Bill stared at me as if I'd grown a third head. "Are you *insane,* Jet?"

"You have a better way? I'm open to suggestions."

"Captain, we'll fall into the river and drown!"

Again with the "captain" stuff. I ignored it; it was a small price to keep Bill placated for a few more hours until we got to the top and—I prayed—found Neil and Samma.

But placated was hardly the word for the boy. Agitated? Panicked? How about psychologically tortured? I had already figured out he had a fear of water, aquaphobia, or whatever it's called. Evidently, if there was anything more terrifying to Bill Hicks than wading *through* waist-high water, it was tightrope-walking *above* the churning, frothy waves. Too bad I wasn't Lewis Carroll's Bellman:

> *"Just the place for a snark," the Bellman cried,*
> *As he landed his crew with care,*
> *Supporting each man on the top of the tide*
> *By a finger entwined in his hair.*

Perhaps if I told Bill three times that we'd make it across, he'd feel better. "What I tell you three times is true."

Even Dwayne looked a bit dubious, although he was eager to give it a try; anything that let him demonstrate his athletic prowess was all right by him. "Of course," he said, rubbing a chin now thickly encrusted with hair, a beard to compliment his Viking mustache—Bill had nothing but a bit of stubble, and he glared in badly disguised jealousy—"it's sort of begging the real question: how do we get the rope across without one of us getting across first?"

"I've already thought of that question."

"How, then?"

"I said I've thought of the question . . . I didn't say I had an answer!" Nobody laughed. Well, *I* thought it was funny! I had to chuckle to make up for my two humorless partners.

"All right," I continued, when no one else said anything, "obviously we have to throw it across somehow."

"How do we make it stick?" At least Dwayne was being helpful; Bill stared mesmerized at the rushing channel, face pale in the waning afternoon sun.

I stared up at where the peak itself was obscured by the shoulder of the mountain. Again, I thought I saw a thin, black line of smoke. "Is that smoke?" I asked, pointing.

"Where?"

"At the top. Could that be Neil and Samma with a signal fire?"

"I can't tell. Maybe. If so, it's not a very good one. If we can't even see it for sure from the base of the mountain, how could anyone see it from a few miles away in an airplane?"

"It's not smoke," said Bill, as if in a daze. "There is no smoke. There's nothing—there's no people left. We're alone; they're all dead."

He was back in his cheery, solipsistic mood. But the more I stared, the more I convinced myself I saw a stream of smoke. "We've got to get up there, Dwayne. I'll bet we'll find the guys, and Neil will know what to do next." That last was true, at least; I'd never known Neil to be stumped by anything, from math to movies. A trivial thing like our survival and restoration to civilization shouldn't tax that giant-sized brain of his.

How could we make the rope stick to the cliff on the other side? "Well, we don't have any Krazy Glue, and it wouldn't work on porous rock anyway. No magnetic clamps, like in science fiction. No suction cups. No huge wad of bubble gum. Well, Dwayne, I guess that just leaves a grappling hook." I didn't actually mean to sound so sarcastic, and I regretted it instantly. I guess the stress was getting to me too, whether I wanted to admit it or not.

Dwayne looked at me, puzzled. "We don't have a grappling hook. Do we, Jeannie?"

I held up my weapon. "I didn't have a javelin or a throwing stick either, Dwayne. We'll *make* one."

Bill gasped, staring at me. "It wouldn't work! Captain, let's just forget the mountain . . . we can't make it across the river. We'll just head toward San Glendora, or wherever the nearest town is!"

I sighed. "Bill, we've been through this. There's *nothing* for twenty or thirty miles, and there's a flooded flood plain in between us and the nearest outpost of a town. We could try going northwest toward Gantry, but we'd have to climb the El Camino mountain range, which is a lot worse than that cliff ahead of us.

"Bill, *this is it,* the only way we can go. Besides, I'm not going to leave Samma and Neil stranded here—not for anything."

He shut his mouth, aware what a coward he sounded. Now his rage was turned on me, and I shuddered. I didn't know how much longer mere logic would keep him in check. Eventually, no matter how much willpower he had, Bill Hicks would not be able to hold out against his inner demons.

I should know; I read all about serial killers in the books that Bill himself lent me. They try to stop the voices or control the urges; they promise themselves over and over that the last killing will be the *last* killing, if they even remember it. But it doesn't work, and they do it again and again and again.

It's a compulsion. I'm not saying they're not responsible—they are. They're evil, pure evil like Miss Gould used to teach me about in Sunday school. But even evil can be helpless to resist the voices.

Eventually, the weight of the horror gets to be too much even for the killer, and he starts leaving little clues, then more and more until finally he's caught— and it's almost always a he; there have been a few female serial killers, like Ulrike Meinhof of the Baader-Meinhof Gang, but not many.

Jeez, there you go again! chastised Miss Taylor, my own inner demon. *You don't have any proof at all that Bill Hicks, your old friend, is any kind of a killer, let alone a twisted serial killer!*

I closed my eyes, feeling dry, silent tears somewhere up inside me. She was right; I didn't have any *proof,* not like you'd need in court.

But I knew. For the first time, I really knew, deep in my heart, that Bill wasn't just a bully, wasn't just a little sick, wasn't even just a rapist.

He had a killer's heart.

Somewhere in his brain, something had snapped a long, long time ago. My heart pounded in retroactive terror as I realized he had been a sociopathic killer even back in the old days, back when I knew him.

The dam inside me burst, and a flood of memories poured forth . . . all the little things I hadn't thought about in years. I didn't suppress them—I don't believe in such a thing as repressed memories; good Lord, if the survivors of the Nazi death-camps remember what happened to them, torment far more horrible than anything imaginable in most people's lives, how could the rest of us repress our daily, minor horrors?

I've never told anyone about this, but I was once molested on a bus. It was super crowded, and I was a twelve-year-old on my first outing alone, going all the way across San Glendora to stay the weekend with my friend Janna Wylie. Anyway, this guy—I'm sure it was a guy, but I never saw him—put his hand on me. The bus was so crowded I couldn't get away. It was several stops before I could squirm far enough away where he couldn't touch me anymore.

I was really upset, crying and stuff; but no one asked me what was wrong, and I probably would have been too ashamed to tell, anyway . . . yeah, like it was my fault. But you're not always thinking right. I told Janna about it, and she put her arms around me and held me for the longest time; then we swore never to tell anyone.

But I've never forgotten it.

And I never forgot all the things Bill Hicks did, either . . . even though I refused to think about them at the time. And you know, it's really a cop-out to say I was just too young to understand. That's bull. I knew what was going on; I was young, but I wasn't stupid! I just didn't want to face up to it. I didn't want to admit that my best friend was sick in the head, psycho. Maybe I thought that would make *me* a psycho for hanging with him.

But he used to touch me all the time, aggressive sex-play—and he didn't care that I didn't want that. He got scarier and scarier . . . he talked about death and dead things, and he said he sometimes died in the middle of the night, then came back to life again.

When we ate lunch together, Bill would describe his sandwiches as human body parts . . . "I'm eating a spleen sandwich today; what do you have?" He was always telling me stories he said he got out of his books on serial killers, but I read almost all of them, and I didn't come across even half the stories Bill told. I think now, and I thought then, he was making most of them up out of his own fetid imagination.

He was a bad one all right. Once, when he was trying to feel my butt, I struggled really hard and shoved him . . . and the little snot *hit* me! He slapped me hard, with a big grin. Without even thinking, I backhanded him in the mouth, drawing blood and knocking him down. It was the last time he hit me;

and from that moment, he suddenly stopped touching me, too.

Come to think of it, that was right around the time I was thirteen and Bill was fourteen, right around puberty. I always wondered whether all of a sudden Bill's drives got too serious even for him, the voices too scary to listen to when he was with me. Maybe he was scared of what he would do to me if he *did* listen.

Well, he was listening now. He cocked his head, like a bird hearing other birds in the forest . . . except I couldn't hear a thing. He bobbed his head up and down a bit; I couldn't tell if it was just a nervous mannerism, or if he was actually agreeing to something.

"Okay," said Dwayne, oblivious to everything that overwhelmed me, "how do we make a grappling hook?"

"What?"

"You said we had to make a grappling hook. How do we make it? We don't have any hooks or anything."

I blinked, hearing the parrot from Huxley's *Brave New World:* "Here and now, boys, here and now!"

"Oh. Grappling hook. Well, it's just some prongs held apart by something, right? Then we tie it to the rope. Let's take a look and see what we can find."

I squatted in the swamp, wishing we were back up in the dry; but there was no way we could climb up that slope we'd just slipped down without launching a major, mountain-climbing expedition; and if we were going to do that, we might as well climb the mountain itself!

I sorted through the flotsam and jetsam we carried and focused on the tent pegs, the only pieces of rigid metal we had. "Somehow we've got to connect these up into a hook," I said, "any suggestions?"

Dwayne scratched his head, confused. Squatting on his haunches and scratching himself, with his bearded face and hairy chest, he looked so much like a gorilla that I burst out laughing.

"What's so hilarious, Jeannie?"

"Never mind! You wouldn't get it."

"Women," he said. "Can't live with 'em. . . ."

I stared at him incredulously, but he insisted on finishing his asinine expression.

"Can't live without 'em."

I rolled my eyes. Jeez, did he think I'd never heard it before? That it was clever?

"Can't put a bullet in 'em," added Bill, staring directly at me.

I looked sharply at the little cockroach, and after a few-seconds staring contest, he dropped his gaze, staring at my chest instead. Plotting. Scheming.

"Uh . . . yeah," said Dwayne, embarrassed for his gender. "I guess. So how did you say we're going to make the tent stakes into a grappling hook?"

We spent the last hour or so of daylight experimenting with grappling-hook designs. I finally found one that I had no trouble describing, but couldn't for the life of me make work in the real world: take a plastic bowl, bore a hole through the bottom, and pass the rope through; tie the stakes together with vines through the eyelets, tie the rope to the vines, and let the stakes drape over the outside of the bowl; tie the stakes tightly against the bowl with vines passing over the open mouth of the bowl.

It sounds complicated, but really it's easy to visualize: you end up with the three tent stakes sticking straight out past the mouth of the bowl, and when you dangle the rope, the whole thing looks like a cupped hand facing up with two missing fingers.

Well, that was the theory, at least; in reality, the stakes could slip, the vines could break, the rope could turn out not to be strong enough to hold the weight of the brave soul who was tightrope-crawling across.

Dwayne worked far into the darkness making the hook; I suggested we wait for light, but he insisted . . . said it kept him busy so he didn't think about all the awful stuff that had happened—and might still be to come.

I would have loved to light a fire, but there was nothing in that gorge that wasn't soaking wet. Fortunately, it wasn't raining, or we probably would have caught double-pneumonia and died before morning.

With the Hag's Tooth due west of us, we had our own, private sunset at seven o'clock, when the shadow of the mountain stretched across us and plunged us into darkness. We took a dinner break around eight, polishing off two pounds of bear meat between us; hiking through trackless wasteland really takes it out of you, calorie-wise.

We crashed at ten-thirty or so, staring up at a sky literally exploding with billions of tiny pinpricks of stellar fusion. Not a cloud and no moon yet; I could almost read by the starlight.

I drifted into an uneasy alliance between sleeping and watching the kaleidoscope above; I dozed, eyelids hovering at half-mast until they fell altogether, and I was sound asleep.

I can't believe I slept right through sunrise; but Dwayne finally had to nudge me awake by shaking my shoulder. I jumped up shouting something about sauerkraut and beehives—but whatever demented land I'd been visiting, it faded so quickly I never did find out what in the world I was talking about.

Bill was awake; I was the only lazy slob. He was chowing down on some of the bear meat . . . but we still had plenty. I'd have killed for a salad bar, though . . . or even sauerkraut (the beehive I could do without).

"How long does it take for a person to start suffering from a lack of vitamins?" I wondered, to nobody in particular.

Bill answered as if I'd asked him. "You shouldn't have a problem in the few days we've been carnivorous. Eventually, we'll have to find a spot to grow vegetables."

"I don't plan to be out here that long, Bill."

"If you start developing problems with your night vision, you've got a serious vitamin A deficiency."

"Thank you, Bill. Now, anybody ready to take a stab at heaving the grappling hook across the river?"

Dwayne grunted; "anybody" meant him, of course. He took the rope and stood at the bank, swinging it back and forth like an Olympic hammer. "What do I throw it at?" he asked.

I shaded my eyes against the sunrise glare reflecting off the cliff and looked for something to take the hook. About fifteen feet up, I saw a lightning-blasted tree trunk. "Aim at the stump; shoot high, so if you miss, it might drop down onto the target anyway."

"Lock phasers," said Bill behind me, falling into another *Star Trek* fugue state.

Dwayne whirled the hook over his head, faster and faster, and suddenly let it fly. It sailed through the air, and my stomach clenched like a fist inside me.

A beautiful, parabolic arc up; a beautiful parabolic arc down. A beautiful miss. The hook fell *way* short, landing in the drink about fifteen feet away from the opposite side. But at least it was fairly on-target.

"Good try, Dwayne!"

"Yeah," added Bill, nastily, "perfect shot. No wonder Johnson High ranks tenth out of fourteen in the track and field conference."

Dwayne turned on the two of us, furious. But I didn't mean anything! Once again, Bill had played an excellent Iago, getting Dwayne p.o.'ed at me, too. Iago was the character in Shakespeare's *Othello, the*

Moor of Venice, who's always playing "let's you and her fight" with Othello and his wife, Desdemona.

"You think you can do better? Fine! You throw the next shot!"

"Dwayne!" I shouted, "the hook! Grab the rope!"

While his back was turned, a log, carried downstream by the rapid current, had snagged our grappling hook and was unreeling the rope faster than I could see. Dwayne turned and stared, frozen.

I jumped past him right into the water, grabbing the tail end of the rope. I tried to plant my feet, but it was like tap-dancing on an ice-skating rink!

I went down, and the freezing snow runoff washed over me. Then something grabbed my long, red hair, and I was enormously grateful that I hadn't gotten it cut short the way my mom wanted.

Dwayne reeled me in like a fish; meanwhile, I wrapped the rope around my hand several times. Just as he hauled me out of the frigid water, the drifting log dislodged itself and continued on its merry way. Yeah, thanks—why couldn't it do that *before* I took an icewater bath?

Seven

Dwayne put his arms around me to warm me, but I decided that wouldn't do my "mighty hunter" image any good. Besides, I had enough trouble with Dwayne calling me Jeannie and expecting us to elope and get married without cuddling up to him in front of psycho-Bill. I shook my head and walked up and down, letting my body heat warm the water slightly. Didn't help much; I still shivered.

Man, I sure wished Neil was here. I wouldn't mind if *he* held me.

That's weird, I thought. Where did *that* come from?

Me and Neil? It was too weird to be true. I must have meant because he was my friend; not like Bill, who had always been a stranger. Maybe that's why we always called him "sir" when we were kids.

"Dwayne, you think you can get it all the way across the river this time?" I asked.

Dwayne stared at the tree stump, then looked down at his incongruous tennis shoes. He shook his head. "It's the wrong shape. It's not like a hammer—that's just a ball on a length of chain. This grappling hook has too much drag ... I can't get it high enough to connect."

"You can't keep it up, eh, Dwayne?" Bill was begging to be pounded again; and again, Dwayne wisely ignored the bait. The big guy wasn't stupid; I think he guessed what Bill had tried to do to me way back when, before I ran off; but since I denied anything happened, for fear that Bill would make good his threat to shoot us both, Dwayne was too much a gentleman to contradict me.

And I think Dwayne was already starting to worry that maybe, just maybe, Bill had a *reason* to feel so secure to hash insults at a guy twice his size. I think Dwayne started to worry about what Bill might or might not have under his coat—*well, join the club, Dwayne*. I'd been worrying about it for days and days.

It's just not that hard to get hold of a gun, if you're determined enough. For heaven's sake, convicts in *prison* can get them.

"So what now?" I asked the invisible sprites.

This time, Dwayne answered. "Well, I guess I've got to get across to those rocks there, about halfway across. From there, it would be easy to hook the tree stump.

I stared at the tiny stepstones he referred to.

An awesome idea . . . the only problem was getting there; you had to leap from rock to rock like Eliza hopping across the ice floes to escape Simon Legree.

And while Dwayne was doing that, I'd be . . . what, entertaining Bill? I looked at the boy quickly; he stared into the middle distance as if not even following the conversation. But his ear happened to be pointed directly toward us, and I knew he was listening.

Oh, peachy. All of a sudden, I remembered that logic problem where a farmer has a fox, a hen, and a sack of feed . . . and I was not about to be left on the bank with the fox while the farmer hopped across the rocks!

"No, Dwayne," I said. "You stay here. I'll go."

"What? Jeannie, that's crazy!"

"Yeah," added Bill, dropping all pretense of inno-cence. "Like Dwayne says, don't be a dweeb."

A dweeb! I got a bit red-faced, then realized Dwayne hadn't *exactly* called me a dweeb; Bill was on a roll. "You're still sick, Dwayne," I improvised. "Amebic dysentery is well-known to affect the inner ear. You could lose your balance, fall into the river, and be swept away."

"Yeah . . ." breathed Bill, visualizing the tragedy and licking his lips.

"Uh—"

"And I'm half your weight, so it's easier for me to jump from rock to rock." That made no sense at all, but I counted on the fact that Dwayne just wasn't used to logical thinking.

"I guess. But—"

"Besides, I want you to tie me off on the other end of the rope and anchor me. I can't anchor you, Dwayne, you weigh about six hundred pounds."

"Two hundred and five."

"I thought you weighed two *twenty*-five?"

"What? Where did you get that idea?"

"Doesn't matter. You can anchor me, but I can't anchor you. It's settled, Dwayne; a lifeboat's got only one captain, and I'm she."

His face reddened, and he puffed and blowed a bit. But in the end, the last argument was the most persuasive: ever since I returned from my sojourn to the wilderness, I was pretty clearly in charge, as much as anyone was. I was "the captain," to use Bill's hallucinatory viewpoint.

"Dwayne," I said, "you're going to have to bring over my pack—I can't carry it while leaping across the rocks. It should be nearly empty, anyway."

Dwayne grunted; I took it as assent.

I tied the hook end of the rope to my belt using a running hitch, so I could get loose if necessary. Then I stood right at the water's edge, hook in hand, staring at the first rock.

It was only about four feet from the bank; I could step to it with my long legs. Gritting my teeth and crouching as low as I could get away with, I made a long leg and landed square.

Unfortunately, I may have been solid, but the rock itself tilted alarmingly under my not inconsiderable weight. Of course, Dwayne's two hundred and five pounds would probably have capsized it, and he'd be sunk already.

I squawked and flapped my arms, like a bird trying to take off. For a few seconds, I honest-to-God thought I was going to take another swim. But I found my balance and concentrated on the next stone.

It was a black rock, flat surface, but resting at a ten-or-fifteen degree slope. And it was seven feet away—the longest jump until I was a third of the way across, when there was a real bitch coming up.

At least it was a big target, about twice the width of a surfboard. I'd had lots of experience balancing on surfboards the summer I spent in Santa Cruz, until I broke my board on a reef at Davenport Beach . . . another reason it made more sense for me to go than Dwayne.

I slid back as far as I dared on my launch pad, feeling it start to roll under my boots. Quickly, before I could wuss-out, I took a running leap and flung myself through the air. I dropped as lightly as an elephant onto the surfboard-rock, and one foot instantly slipped out from under me. My knee slammed into the rock, and for a heartbeat, I thought I'd shattered my kneecap!

Bad pain. Lots of pain. But I got to my feet, and it just throbbed; if it was a break, it was only a hairline fracture. I could still stand on it. When I was in a more stable position, I'd be sure to cross my fingers that nothing was broken.

Dwayne shouted something encouraging from the bank. Over the rushing water, it sounded like "No taco take-out, Jeannie!" I couldn't help smiling and didn't even try to figure out what he'd really said; I liked no taco take-out better.

The next two rocks were pretty easy; just a step farther out, then another. But at last, I came to the true monster: a jump of nearly *ten feet,* longer than I'd ever jumped a standing broad jump before. Probably not a world's record, but it may as well have been.

My target was a small, mini-mountain itself: It stuck up about three feet from the surface of the river, but was slick from spray and covered with algae and lichen.

There was just no good way to make the jump. I could do a running broad jump of a lot more than ten feet . . . but here, I couldn't run and I couldn't land.

I swallowed hard; the only thing I could think of doing was to actually *dive* for the rock headfirst, and try to grab it with my hands before I was washed seventy miles downriver into San Francisco Bay.

I looked back at the boys. Dwayne shouted something else, but this time I couldn't hear a thing. I realized he hadn't figured out what I faced.

But Bill knew; he was watching me with the most blood-chilling, marrow-freezing expression . . . like he was watching an ant climb up a candle, betting with himself whether it would crawl into the flame and incinerate itself.

He held a half-smile, face flushed with excitement, leaning forward at the waist . . . a kid at the circus waiting to see if a lion bites the trainer's head off. Bill saw what I had in front of me; and he knew I didn't exactly have a great chance of pulling it off.

I turned back, bitter. The betrayal was complete. Whatever last vestige of doubt I had about Bill Hicks sank into the river. He was a dangerous, sick boy when I knew him—and he was a dangerous, sick man now.

I decided I was going to make it across . . . just to spite Bill.

I focused my concentration entirely on the rock. I was about to do something no rock climber ever does: lunge for a handhold, totally off-balance. If I missed, I was going to have to depend on Dwayne to haul me in before I drowned, because there was no way I could swim in that current.

I relaxed. I matted out all sounds and sights except for my target. Then I crouched—and leapt.

I don't know what happened . . . it was the greatest jump of my life. I knew I had it right on target. I was going to land on all fours on the rock, quadrupling my chance of catching hold of something.

Then almost to the rock, the rope suddenly snapped tight. That *gentleman* Dwayne hadn't given me enough slack!

The suddenly taut rope yanked me short, and I fell facefirst into the frigid water—facefirst onto the rock. My fingers slammed hard against a rocky outcropping, and my fingers felt like they'd all broken! But I grabbed and squeezed tight anyway, despite the agony.

My body was instantly grabbed by the moving mass of water, and at once I felt like I was dangling from a cliff with a hundred-pound pack hanging from my shoulders. It was just the weight of the water— thank God I didn't have a *real* pack on my back!

I can do maybe two pull-ups when I'm fresh and rested. If I kip, I can do five. But this was different . . . the water tore at me with greedy hands, trying to pull me from the rock by main force.

I discovered another problem: when I hit the icy river, I was startled into exhaling . . . and now I realized I was out of air and trapped under a ton of rushing water.

Terror gave me desperate strength. I don't know where it came from, but I managed to pull my chin up to hook over my hands.

My stretching legs brushed against another rock, too small to break the surface of the swollen river. I just got my toe against it, then found a closer rock for my left foot. I was climbing again . . . sideways.

I started to hear a pounding in my ears and saw sparkles. I needed air, like yesterday! Then, with a final kick, my head broke the surface and I sucked oxygen like a vacuum cleaner.

But I had no time to sit and rest: in water as cold as that was, high thirties or low forties, you have only a few minutes before you die of exposure . . .

water sucks away your heat a lot faster than air does!

Now that I could see—out of one eye, at least —I grabbed for hand- and footholds as fast as I safely could and struggled up onto the rock. I started to hyperventilate, this time for the stupidest reason: one of my eyes was totally blurry, and I was worried my contact lens had been washed away!

I started to whimper—totally un-captainlike. I was wildly grateful that no one could see me from back on the riverbank; I'd have had to turn in my epaulets, or whatever captains wear.

Then I closed both eyes and took five deep, long breaths. The most important thing to do when I have an anxiety attack was to control my breathing; once I got control of that, I could usually argue myself out of it.

This time, I didn't need to; while I was breathing, I started blinking my eyes, and the right eye came back into focus. The lens had just been rotated, not lost. I have an astigmatism, and rotation totally bags the focus.

The adventure felt like it took a couple of months at least; but in reality, they all happened in—sorry—the blink of an eye. When I calmed down and figured out where the heck I was—in the middle of a river freezing my boots off clinging to a rock blinking my eyes and breathing heavily—only a few seconds had passed.

Then I realized the "crowning" touch: on top of everything else, I'd chipped off half my right upper incisor.

Shaking a bit from the adrenaline rush, I scrambled out of the water and up the rock. Only after I got on top did I remember that the whole point of the exercise was to hurl the grappling hook at the tree stump . . . I felt around behind me and almost panicked again: the hook was gone!

Then I looked down, and there it was; my rope belt had spun around, and the hook was in front, bouncing off my bruised kneecaps; if I weren't so numb from the freezing water, I'd have felt it.

As I unhooked the hook from around my middle, I started to feel annoying butterflies in my stomach, and my ears buzzed. I tried to ignore it; I thought it was just residual from the panic attack. But it got worse, and I realized I was afraid.

I hadn't been this worried when it was just my own life, like when I was trying to learn to hunt, or even when the scene was morphing faster than I could follow, like when the bear charged me.

But now, I had the time to sit back and listen to Miss Taylor say, *Girl, you could totally let down everyone else. You could miss, lose the hook, totally lose everything. Everyone's depending on you!*

I wanted to swallow, but I had no saliva. If only my mouth were as wet as my palms! If only I had my tooth, the whole tooth.

All right, you caught me: when I'm really, really freaked, I make jokes. Yeah, like you hadn't figured that out already. That's how I sort of cope.

I looked back . . . big mistake. Bill was still staring

at me like a gargoyle, and Dwayne Cors, professional boy-jock, was pantomiming throwing a grappling hook, as if maybe I'd forgotten what I was supposed to do and needed encouragement. Men!

I turned back and stared at the stump. I'd been so offhand, so confident about being able to loop it while I was standing back on semidry land on the marshy riverbank. Yeah, it'd be so easy; I'd toss it in between yawns.

But now that I stood here, the thirty feet looked more like three hundred. I remembered trips to the shooting range with my father, before he—I discovered that even at fifteen feet, it was pretty darned easy to point the .45 just *slightly* left or right and miss the paper entirely!

And with the hook, it was even worse. I had to twirl the thing and let go at just the right moment to make it go forward instead of straight up (after which it would land right on my head, like a cartoon, of course) . . . and somehow aim it laterally at the same time!

Suddenly, I had new respect for Dwayne's try. It was way short—but it was on-target, which was more than I could guarantee.

Clenching my teeth to stop them from chattering (I told myself it was just the chill), I started spinning the hook. It was nice and clumsy, like swinging a cat around by its tail. My tongue explored the gaping hole in my smile . . . Jeez, I sure hoped we could find a good dentist, or periodontist, or whatever it was.

Now or never, Jeanette, I thought.

I didn't let go.

This is it, girl—bombs away!

I didn't let go.

All right, on the count of three . . . one, two—

Wait, on the count of ten: ten, nine, eight, seven, six, five, four, three, two . . .

Next time around—one, two, here we go!

All right, on the next good swing.

My arm started to ache, and the swing got raggedy. That was a good excuse to stop and think about it. I knelt on the rock, massaging my shoulder.

It was silly. All I had to do was throw a stupid hook thirty feet on top of a tree stump! I could do it in my stocking feet with both hands tied behind my back . . . well, you know what I mean.

The more I thought about it, the madder I got. I was totally steamed! I was acting just like what I hated, like a g*i*r*l . . . not like a *grrl*. There was a time for girls, and a time for grrls. This wasn't girl-time.

I turned neon red; the flush started on the back of my neck and spread to my face, and then I felt it all over my body. Everyone was staring at me, I just knew it! And they were all saying, "Man, we shoulda never sent a *girl* to do a man's job." I could just hear Bill sneering and Dwayne being so polite, so gentle-manly, so *infuriating*.

That did it. I wasn't going to stand by and hear my entire gender maligned by a bunch of sexist dweebs, even if the whole conversation was in my mind!

I stood abruptly, and before I could even think about what I was doing and start having doubts—that was my mistake last time—I wound up, swirled the hook a couple of times to get the heft, and let it go at the bottom of its arc!

It sailed through the air . . . and would you believe it? Bull's-eye, right over the tree stump!

Hah! You shouldn't believe everything you hear. I missed; the range was good, but I was about a yard off downstream, to the left.

The metal and vine monstrosity plunked into the water and started to drift away. I held tight and reeled it in . . . and when I retrieved it, I lost all fear of failure. I'd failed, thank God, and now I was free to try and fail and eventually succeed.

You know, failure is pretty underrated in our society. I don't mean to interrupt everything with some airhead, philosophical psychobabble, but this is like important, and I just realized it that moment.

The right to fail is the most important inalienable right we have. When they take away people's right to fail, say by being so worried about our "self esteem" if we aren't absolutely perfect at everything first time out of the box that they tell us failure is really success . . . well, they might as well stick a disk in our heads with the program USELESS.EXE on it. Look: I failed, and once I realized I had the right to try *and fail,* I chilled; then I got mad, and damn it, after six more tries, I succeeded!

And no one had to give me a gold medal for tripping, like on that totally uncool *Sesame Street* episode I saw while baby-sitting Janna Wylie's little nephew.

Yup, there I stood with a stupid expression on my face, staring at the rope that was unexpectedly attached to one tree stump ten yards away.

I unhooked the rope from my middle. Acting way cool, like I'd known from the first moment that I could do it, I turned back to the boys and made a circle with my arm, touching my head in the international scuba-diver's symbol for "stoked." After a moment, I realized that probably neither of them was a scuba diver, but they seemed to figure it out.

Dwayne backed away, playing out the rope until he had his back to the slope we'd descended . . . or fallen down, to be brutal. He had his pick of tree roots sticking out of the mud to attach to.

I couldn't exactly see what he was doing, but I hoped he remembered how I had made a stopper knot and slipped it into the crotch of a tree branch, so we could retrieve the rope later. I squinted . . . and ground my teeth; it sure looked like the overlarge dorkjock had simply tied the rope into a knot around the roots! I guess being a National Merit finalist didn't necessarily translate into being street smart, or river-crossing smart.

He had at least tied the rope high and tight enough that it was well out of the water . . . though how well it would hold the weight of a human, I couldn't guess. It wasn't a mountain-climbing rope, and I had no idea how heavy it was rated.

But I did know one thing: the first person across the final gap of river had better be me. Someone had to make it to the other side and find a more permanent, safer anchor for that end of the rope.

That meant I would have to rely not only on the stump and the rope, but also on the stupid vines that held the hook together. And on my throwing skill: was the hook *really* solid, or was it held just by a couple inches of tent peg?

I held onto the rope, head height, with both hands and slowly put my hundred and whatever pounds of weight on it. It sagged alarmingly, but not quite all the way to the river. I hooked my long legs up and over and dangled for a few seconds; it *felt* steady, but I hadn't even started to move yet.

I was about to find out just how solid it really was.

Eight

You swing your right leg on the *outside* of the rope and hook it around to the right, all the way over the rope; then you hook your foot under the rope again. Your left foot steps down on the top of your right foot, trapping the rope between your feet.

Now you can press hard to push yourself along the rope, or lighten up to draw your legs up. You might recognize this foot grip: it's the same one you're supposed to use to *climb* a rope, just done horizontally instead. In fact, it's also pretty much what the catcher in a trapeze act does, except he loops one leg around each rope of his trapeze.

I did this because I was afraid to dangle by my hands; I wanted to lock my arms around the rope and use my feet because I was dead-tired from ice floe leaping and shivering from the cold.

I inched my way toward the opposite bank,

shuddering a bit when I left my rock; from thereon, I had the rope and nothing but the rope.

My gut tightened, and I stared down at the water . . . which was another mistake, sort of like looking straight down when you're free-climbing a thirty-foot face. I got scared; that water looked like it was going about sixty miles per hour, and frothing like detergent in the washing machine!

I closed my eyes to better concentrate on my footing, and humped across the rope like an upside-down caterpillar.

I was so into the Zen of tightrope crawling that I didn't even see the stump coming; I thumped my head against it and opened my eyes in surprise . . . I made it!

"I made it!" I shouted, not caring that nobody could hear a word.

Just as I said the words, I heard a terrible ripping noise, and the whole stump tore loose from the soil!

I did what any smart girl would do: I squawked and let go, my body dropping heavily into the muddy bank. I could have lost the rope—wouldn't that have been a bitch! Getting the rope across was the whole point of this exercise. But as fate would have it, the fact that I'd looped it around my leg saved me from a lifetime of regrets. I grabbed the hook before the rope had a chance to fully unwind from my leg.

> *O Fortuna!*
> *Velup luna,*
> *Statu variabilis,*

Semper crescis
Aut decrescis.

The famous, or infamous paean to *Luck, Empress of the World,* written by some truly mad monkish troubadour and popularized by Carl Orff in *Carmina Burana.* I could think of no better way of putting it; sure wish I knew what it meant, but Latin isn't a part of the curriculum at Andrew Johnson.

I held the hook tight and climbed the bank; about ten feet further was a more solidly rooted tree . . . it would have to do; there wasn't any more rope left. I tied it off with a strong square knot, looping the end through again to lock it. I gave the boys the high-sign again, and Dwayne returned it. Bill was too busy wrapping his arms around himself and staring at the water; he didn't see me.

I put my hand to my mouth and brought it away dripping blood. An instant surge of adrenaline gave me another mini-anxiety attack (and nausea) . . . but I knew what it was this time. Shaking and trying to slow my respiration, I washed out my mouth with river water, not even caring what microorganisms might be swimming around in there (Dwayne's giant amebas, et cetera).

I have to admit I felt a little twinge of revenge at that slime, Bill Hicks. Let him suffer! I half-hoped he would become so terrified of the river that he would let go and fall into the very water he was so afraid of.

Then I realized I might be making enemies upstairs
by wishing Bill dead.

In the situation we were in, I sure didn't want to
burn any bridges; we needed all the help we could
get. I had never paid much attention in Sunday
school, or in church, for that matter. In fact, my
mother didn't even like me attending, and I told her I
only went so I could meet some outlaw biker and
elope. But now I wasn't so sure . . . maybe it was that
old thing about there being no atheists in foxholes?
Well, I wasn't quite in a foxhole, and I wasn't quite
ready to be ordained . . . but I guess I was thinking
more about it than I ever had before.

I apologized just in case anyone heard me and
resolved not to try to hex Bill into plunging into the
raging waters.

Dwayne began remonstrating with Bill, pointing at
the rope and making broad gestures . . . I concluded
he was trying to get Bill to climb across next. Bill
stood frozen, hugging himself, staring at the water.

Dwayne gave up and turned to the rope; but just
then, Bill snapped out of his phobia—or into another
fantasy world—and dropped his arms, standing totally normal. In fact, he sauntered past the startled jock
to the tightrope, negligently brushing past Dwayne.

Bill, if he were still Bill and not some other, psycho personality at that moment, casually hooked one
leg over the rope, holding on with both hands. Then
he started to pull himself across, hand over hand.

"You're insane!" I yelped. he couldn't hear me, of

course; it was a rhetorical interjection. He continued on, a bland smile on his face, as if he were a character in a movie and he had already seen how the scene ended.

He carried his pack on his belly; I don't know how he managed to reach around it with those stubby arms.

When he was halfway across, he started to tire. I guess even the most disturbed mind can't completely ignore bodily fatigue . . . just like the immortal kid who didn't even need to eat, wolfed down a huge pile of forest mushrooms a few days earlier.

But he simply switched legs in a dangerous, heart-stopping maneuver that I never would have tried, and kept right on going. Yeesh!

The rope held him okay. Not surprising . . . he couldn't be that much heavier than I, maybe twenty or thirty pounds (I was never very good at guessing weight, not even my own). The real test would be when two-hundred-and-twenty-five-pound Dwayne, who insisted he was a mere two-oh-five, toddled across.

Then in two zips and a slide, Bill dropped off the rope and stood staring at me, chuckling indulgently. I was half-afraid he would reach across and pat my head.

This was exactly the position I most didn't want to be in! I was the chicken left on the wrong side of the river with only the fox for company.

"Nice, uh, job," I said. "Coming across, I mean."

"Yes, wasn't it? I didn't want to leave you standing there too long alone, Jet."

I really, *really* hated it when he called me that. I sort of felt like it was Neil's copyright. And Bill knew it, too; I wasn't fooled. He wore a mask of caring and concern; but behind it was really a raging, aggressive attack-attorney, ready to rip me away on cross-examination.

I decided I'd better take control . . . otherwise, I'd have an unleashed feral dog on my hands. "Check that knot, will you? I want to make sure it's tight before Dwayne starts coming across."

Bill—Beta-Bill, the Other—looked cryptically at me, a half-smile creeping across his lips. "Too late. Here he comes now. He'll just have to sink or swim, depending on the whims of the gods."

I looked, thus losing momentum and authority to Bill Hicks. He was right: Dwayne was already several feet out on the rope. I ground my teeth when I saw he was carrying only one pack—his own. Men!

He had both legs hooked up and over the line, and was crawling with slow, steady determination . . . he didn't have either my experience with ropes or Bill's multiple personalities, one for every occasion. Dwayne kept stopping and staring down at the water, scant inches below him.

The rope bowed alarmingly under his weight, and the further he got, the worse it stretched. Less than halfway across, he was already skimming the frothy waves—and it was only going to get worse.

In fact, he wasn't going to make it at all!

I gasped; Dwayne was already kicking up his own rooster tail in the heavy current . . . he was being battered—any minute, he would lose his grip and be swept away. Leaving me alone with Bill in the wasteland.

We had to do something quick to raise him up a few inches—just six inches would do it! "Bill," I barked, "grab the line! Help me pull!"

Bill started to object; he *liked* being in psychic control. But urgency filled me with the iron will of a drill instructor, and Bill jumped to obey even before he realized what was happening. I guess I wasn't good at faking it; but when the real thing struck, authority gusted through me like a divine zephyr, blowing away the stupid masks.

Bill grabbed the rope, and I grabbed hold right behind him. Straining, we pulled backward, stretching the line tighter until we pulled Dwayne up and out of the water.

The strain was unbelievable . . . I thought my back was going to break! For an instant, that—that *boy* stopped, wondering how he'd suddenly levitated half a foot above the water! Then light dawned on marblehead, and he started crawling as fast as guts and adrenaline could push him.

The rope started to slip through my sweaty palms. "I—I can't hold it anymore!" I shouted. Bill said nothing, but his feet started slipping. He tried to back up.

Two seconds later, my hands involuntarily relaxed, letting the rope slide through. Pulled off-balance, Bill slipped and fell face-forward in the mud.

Dwayne dropped back down, kicking up some more spray; but then he rebounded up again, just barely out of the water.

We'd done it . . . we'd held him up just long enough!

Still in high gear, even though the danger was past, Dwayne double-timed the last thirty feet and dropped off next to Bill in the saturated soil.

I put my hands on my hips, staring down at my crew. I had to say something fast to maintain the illusion. "Well, boys . . . you going to lie there forever? Or are we going to find a semidry spot to camp for the night?"

The words had the desired effect: Dwayne groaned and sat up, grumbling but back in control. And Bill went back to being Alpha-Bill, shifty-eyed and sullen but not openly homicidal. So long as I could keep *that* personality uppermost, I would have no trouble handling him. But I had a cold feeling in my gut that Beta-Bill was becoming stronger . . . and that sooner or later, I'd have to confront him.

"Semidry" turned out to be as elusive as desert same. The cliff was virtually straight up and down; but at the base, it bent inward, finally hitting no flatter than a fifteen-degree slope when it hit the river. The rains had thoroughly soaked the mountain, then run off into the sloping ground, which could never dry because it was angled and in shadow half the day.

Everywhere we walked, my feet made sucking sounds in the mud, and every step pulled up huge clods of soil. Finally, the best we could do was find a reasonably big tree whose branches gave us a little shelter in case the ominous clouds above us opened up and dumped another pail of water.

We dumped the packs—the *two* packs—on the ground, and I turned on Dwayne with righteous anger. I can go from zero to bitch in three-point-five seconds! I had just opened my mouth when that boyjock casually opened his pack and dumped mine out of it.

I stood there opening and closing my mouth like a guppy for a few seconds.

Dwayne noticed me. "What?" he asked, confused.

"We, ah, better get the rope," I finished. Lame-o!

Returning to the bank, I untied my end of the rope and gave an experimental tug. Nothing.

Of course not; it had held Dwayne's weight—I wasn't going to dislodge it by yanking no it, not by myself! Dwayne and I tried, then Dwayne and Bill and I.

I stared at the football hero. "You tied a square knot, didn't you?"

"Well sure. It's the strongest knot, isn't it?"

"What Jet's trying to say," sneered Bill, "is that your head is the strongest knot. How are we supposed to get the rope back now, big man?"

Dwayne looked hangdog; but I'd been thinking. "Actually no, that's not what I mean, Bill. We're alive, and we're across; and if Dwayne hadn't tied the rope as tight as he did, we might be neither."

To punctuate my words, I gave a final tug on the rope. With a crack like a rifle shot, the tree branch Dwayne had tied the rope to snapped off, and the line fell limp. Startled, I recovered and quickly reeled in the rope before the branch could catch on any flotsam in the river.

They both looked at me, Bill in fury and Dwayne in relief; me, I couldn't stop laughing. Bill stomped back to the camp, if you want to call it such. After a few silent seconds, we joined him.

We braced our feet against the tree trunk and tried to sleep as best we could—with the prospect of rolling over in our sleep and sliding feetfirst into the churning rapids.

I dozed fitfully, which means I kept waking up with a start, a thousand percent convinced I was on my way into the big muddy. Dwayne did the same; we caught each other awake a few times. But Bill passed out like he'd taken a double-dose of Nytol and lay still as death, not even snoring, until dawn.

Groggy and still tired, Dwayne and I struggled up to a sitting position to watch the sun rise over the eastern range. *If we'd followed the original plan,* I thought, *that's where we'd be . . . with a dozen helicopters looking for us. Or rather, with NO ONE looking for us, since we would have arrived back home safely yesterday!*

Out here, there were probably a dozen vultures looking for us, but no Search-and-Rescue (SAR) helos, planes, or flying saucers. We had only one chance: get to the highest mountain—the Hag's Tooth—and burn something that made a lot of smoke. Maybe we'd attract a wandering plane . . . everybody in the county must know we were missing by now.

Of course, that's exactly what Neil and Samma had been doing for several days now—if that was them up on the peak. If my eyes weren't playing tricks on me.

Whether they are or aren't, said Miss Taylor, *you'd still better get up there and find something to burn.* She was always most active just before I went to sleep and just after I woke up.

I looked at Bill and suddenly realized my fantastic fortune . . . *he was asleep and I was awake!* My groggy brain finally woke to the fact that I finally had my chance to see just exactly what he was carrying . . . and if it was a gun, to take it away from him.

Holding my breath, I reached across and gently lifted his jacket. He moaned and twitched, and I froze.

I stayed frozen in a tableau for what seemed a couple of hours—ten seconds, probably. Then the boy sighed deeply.

I lifted the coat just enough to peek underneath. Nothing…Nothing? How could that be?

Oh. The backpack; of course!

I rolled to my knees and crawled silently to Bill's pack. But just as I reached for it, Dwayne reached over and—I couldn't believe it!—*shook Bill awake.*

A lesser mortal would have jumped back guiltily from the pack, trying to look innocent. But not I. I knew beyond any doubt that this was my one and only chance. He might be awake, but I was closer to the pack than he was, and nothing could stop me in time.

Bill blinked, then suddenly saw what I was doing. "Hey, get away from that!" he exclaimed, wasting time by waiting to see if I would pull away. When he realized I had no intention of listening, Bill lunged for his pack . . . but I was there first!

He grabbed at my arms, and I didn't bother trying to dislodge him; I yanked open the pack, accidentally upending it in the process. A bunch of crap spilled out, crazy things: plant samples, a rat or squirrel skull, dirty clothes, a harmonica (I didn't even know he played), a pinecone, a safety razor (not that he really had use for that), about a hundred different prescription medicines, nail clippers, a pair of hand-cuffs (!), and . . . well, I won't describe it. A pleasure device. My cheeks turned crimson just looking at it.

And no gun. Repeat, *no gun.* The little weasel had been BS'ing us all along.

"Whoops!" I said. "I thought this was *my* pack."

Bill, Beta-Bill, said nothing; he just stared, cold and remote. The irises of his eyes shrunk to tiny, reptilian dots: *you are a dead girl,* they said. *You will never leave this mountain alive.*

I stopped breathing for a moment, lost in those eyes. That wasn't just the thousand-yard stare of a killer, like Bundy or Manson. There was something infinitely more evil inside what used to be Bill—what was *always* Bill, though I never really recognized him when I was young.

He didn't just want to kill me. Bill Hicks wanted to swallow my soul. If he'd been a ghoul, he would have sucked my life force dry in a heartbeat.

But he was just a man, a boy, really; and things like vampires and ghouls exist only in our sick imaginations. There was nothing he could do; my soul was my own.

I started to help Bill get his things back into the pack, but he smiled so viciously that I faltered and sat back, allowing him to clean up on his own. His face was red, even redder than mine had been, seeing that thing he was carrying. Maybe he was embarrassed that *I* had seen it. I could understand Samma carrying it, but *Bill?* A guy? Oh well . . . no accounting for taste. I guess some people do take both paths.

I considered relieving him of the handcuffs, but I couldn't think of a good excuse; I didn't want Dwayne to begin doubting my sanity. If he and Bill double-teamed me, that would be the end.

I stood, bracing myself against the slope. Putting my hand on my knife hilt, I issued marching orders.

"We're going up the cliff, guys. We'll use the rope, even though it's not rated, not a mountaineering rope, and probably stretched out from crossing the river and getting wet. But it's all we've got."

Dwayne stared up the cliff face, face growing whiter as he craned his neck further. "That must be a hundred feet!" he objected.

"Not even half that to the ledge," I said. "Fifty feet tops. And it's a rough cliff; looks like there are a lot of handholds and ledges to stand on.

"All right, boys, listen up. We can't afford any macho crap and bullroar, no fancy stuff. We're all total amateurs at this—I've taken a couple of classes, but that's it—so don't make like Stallone in that mountain-climbing movie, what was it, *Cliffhanger.* No leaping from crag to crag.

"Dwayne, you've got point. You're the strongest man here, and you did pretty well last time." We had climbed partway up a ninety-foot cliff at night, no more than forty feet; then Bill froze. We tried to get him to move . . . then he lunged blind for a handhold that was out of his reach.

Bill had dropped, pulling Dwayne and me off the mountain and into the polluted water below.

"Then me," I continued, "and Bill last." I was thinking that with the rope pulling him inexorably upward, maybe he wouldn't freeze again.

"I don't want to go last," he grumbled. "I want second. I don't demand to be first. Second is fine. You wouldn't begrudge me that, would you? I lost my dog, you know."

His babbling gave me ice-cube creeps up my spine. Then Bill narrowed his eyes and stepped menacingly toward me, curling his lip in disgust.

I should have backed up; I sure did a week earlier! But maybe I'd just had enough. And now that I knew two of Bill's secrets, one of which was that he did *not* have a .38, something just snapped inside of me.

I stared him down as he stood face to chin with me, and I put my hand on the pommel of my knife.

Bill caught the movement and hastily backed up a few steps; then, when his brain caught up, and he realized I'd backed him away with my knife, without even drawing it, he became angry and embarrassed. He stared at my blade as if it were a poisonous snake.

Then he smiled. I didn't like the smile; but for the moment, at least, I had the upper hand.

I didn't realize how quickly that could change.

Nine

Up the airy mountain,
Down the rushy glen
We daren't go a-hunting,
For fear of little men. . . .

William Allingham was talking about *The Fairy Folk*, but that first half-stanza seemed to apply pretty well to our own evil elf, Bill Hicks.

We busied ourselves fooling with the ropes and things; I used the same knot I'd used the last time—nothing wrong with the bowline on a coil. In fact, without any equipment, harnesses, or carabiners, it was about all I could do. I tried to forget the emetic descriptions I'd read of climbers who had their ribs broken and their internal innards rearranged by roping themselves up directly.

I spoke quietly to Dwayne, last-minute pep talk: "Look, killer, try to remember you've got a couple of people behind you who aren't six-foot-nineteen and don't bench-press Yugos for a hobby. Pick the easiest route you can . . . we're looking to get to the top in one piece—well, three pieces—not to score points. And above all, keep moving; there's a ledge about forty or fifty feet up, I think; we can rest there."

"Forty feet, gotcha. Piece of cake. What's my reward if I get us there?"

"How about a piece of cake? All right, all right; if you bring us all up to the ledge, I'll . . . give you a big, wet kiss. In the quad, during lunch. With everyone standing around and watching."

And hooting. Okay, it was worth *one* kiss to get us out safely.

"Hah, you already owe me one of those!"

"What? I do not!" He was talking about the last time we tried to scale the Hag's Tooth, our less-than-auspicious debut on the west face. But he misremembered. "I said you'd get a French kiss if you got us to the top safely."

"Or *bottom,* Jeannie! You said top or bottom safely."

"We fell off!"

"Yes, but *safely.* We're alive, aren't we?"

Whoops . . . I started to remember that he was probably right. "Well, two kisses? Wait, this is becoming more serious than I meant. Dwayne, I was just trying to motivate you to the top, like that girl in *The Eiger Sanction*—except I wasn't about to open my shirt for you."

He struggled visibly. His gentlemanly side kept

trying to get the rest of him to say, "It's all right, I know you were just kidding," But all that came out was, "Yeah, okay, so you still owe me *one* French kiss." He shrugged. Well, he might be a gentleman, but he was also a seventeen-year-old boy, and they take longer to mature than girls. You have to make allowances.

Besides, even if kissing Dwayne right on the—on the quad wasn't my idea of the decorous thing to do, it wouldn't hurt my non-existent reputation any.

Suddenly, a shape loomed up behind me. Bill, of course. He stood right up against me and leaned over to whisper in my ear, "Jet, I think you'd better get an oral history before you start swapping bodily fluids with Dwayne . . . I'm just worried about your health. This isn't a bag, but, you know, he *has* been with a lot of girls—and I heard that Stephanie Hopper had to go to the clinic several times last summer."

For an instant, hot anger flooded me: how dare that simian Dwayne trick me down the same wet path followed by her, the bird-slut of Alcatraz? Steph Hopper should change the E in her first name to an A! I opened my mouth to berate Dwayne for even thinking of me and Hopper in the same breath, when suddenly Miss Taylor, who had been frantically signaling, broke through the static: *Damn it, girl, he did it to you again!*

I forcibly calmed myself as Bill stepped back; he made a point of brushing me, touching me again, as if it were just an accident. I didn't like it—who wants to be touched by a killer creep?—but at least it was better than the totally brazen way he was grabbing me earlier, whenever Dwayne wasn't looking.

Dwayne's ears burned red; I know he heard. But he didn't say anything or defend himself. Did that mean it was true, that he'd been with Hopper and she later had to get some shots? Maybe he was a weasel after all.

And there lay Bill's true power, the power of every Iago: Even when you *know what he's doing,* it still works! You still end up with doubts. What a slime. I was ashamed for having called him a longtime friend, even a few days earlier.

"Ready, Dwayne?" I asked. He nodded and addressed the cliff.

He started to climb right away; then he stopped, and instead spent a couple of minutes planning a route up the face. "Good, Dwayne," I encouraged. "You climb with your brain, not your hands."

When he started up again, it was an easy path—the same one I'd picked out while we were roping up. He started deviating about five feet up, which was to be expected: there are more ways up a mountain than there are climbers. The right way is whatever way gets you to the top.

I let him gain about ten feet on me, then I started up. I wanted to give him room to climb, but still have some faint prayer of stopping him if he lost it, or at least turning it into a controlled fall, scraping the face

of the cliff to avoid total free-fall. Besides, I wanted a
little slack in the rope between us, or I'd be tripping
over it every time I shifted left or right.

Bill jumped onto the cliff directly behind me, so
close I almost kicked his head when my foot slipped
momentarily; it was really distracting . . . I wished he
would give me as much room as I was giving
Dwayne. Being so close, the rope looped down past
Bill, then back up to his waist . . . a perfect opportuni-
ty to get tangled. But there was no point in saying
anything. Bitter experience taught me you couldn't
tell Bill anything.

Besides, climbing was harder work than I remembered. I'd been earthbound too long, and my grip was
weak and my balance shaky. My mind wandered . . . I
caught myself remembering the old days with Neil
instead of focusing totally on the here and now.

Abruptly, I was yanked back to the present when
the climbing got much tougher. Above us, the cliff
bulged outward, something I hadn't seen from
below. We were up about twenty feet, enough to be
jarring if we fell, but not enough to kill us. Evidently,
the platform I saw was on the top side of a bulge.

Dwayne still seemed all right, so I didn't say anything; no need to worry him or scare him into being
unable to continue.

Bill slipped a couple of times, and each time I
braced myself; but he caught himself and continued.
He was clearly the weakest climber of us three . . .
and he paid the least attention to what he was doing.

He'd disappeared yet again into his own private universe, one where he was the captain and the rest of the world was his starship.

I'd never climbed a slope greater than ninety degrees before; it was extremely tiring. I couldn't lean against the rock and rest. Even though the slope was only a few degrees past vertical, I dangled from the cliff constantly, tiring my arms. But I didn't dare lean against the rope, either; Dwayne was strong, but he wasn't experienced.

A half-hour passed; it was hard work, essentially free-climbing the cliff. Dwayne stopped a couple of times when he lost the route. Both times he had to back down and shift to the right.

I tried to help Bill as much as I could, pointing out the hand- and footholds I'd used. He mostly ignored me.

I was pretty damned glad we were nearing the platform. I desperately needed the rest.

"Can you see it yet?" I called up to Dwayne. He didn't answer, so I repeated myself.

Finally he called back, "See what?"

"The plateau, the platform! What we're climbing for—can you see it above you?"

Long pause. "I don't see anything. Are you sure we're in the right place?"

I risked a look down, lining myself up by the stand of three trees in a straight line, where we'd spent the night. "Right place—we're about forty feet up, right altitude. Are you sure you don't see anything?"

Dwayne's silence was eloquent.

"Dwayne . . . please tell me you see a plateau where we can rest. Even if you don't see anything, tell me you do!"

"Jeannie, I'm sorry. I don't see a thing but more cliff."

I hung by my aching hands, horror spreading across my brain. I'd been so much relying on what I *thought* I'd seen, that I was almost ready to deliberately drop at the thought that there would be no rest until we got to the top. This was no better than the west face! Damn that Geological Survey anyway—what were they smoking when they drew that lying map?

Chagrined, I realized what must have happened: the outward bulge threw off my perspective from the ground. I was obviously staring at a nearly vertical cliff face, but it looked like a plateau next to the outward-leaning part.

If I were still in shape, I wouldn't worry much. But my hands throbbed and my calves were already starting to tremble, and we'd only climbed forty feet! I was sweating like a horse, panting with exertion, and we had another forty feet to go!

I was totally humiliated. Here I was, the one who whipped everybody to this side of the mountain because the climb was *easier.* But here we were, facing a straight climb of another four stories before we got to a slope gentle enough that we could, with difficulty, walk.

My skin tingled unpleasantly. What was I supposed to say to Dwayne and Bill? Whoops, sorry? Obviously, my much-vaunted memory had totally failed me: whatever mountain I remembered as having a gentle east face, it wasn't the Hag's Tooth.

Damn it!

"Better keep on, Dwayne," I called up. "It's a lot harder climbing down than up, and we have to get up to a resting point. If we try to stay here any longer, we'll fall."

Wordlessly, he started again. Even Dwayne was blowing hard; I could hear him all the way down where I was. Then he climbed past the bulge, and I couldn't see him anymore, and wouldn't until I passed it myself in a few minutes.

I looked down and saw Bill way below me, at the end of his rope. He was having a hard time, not quite frozen, but just a few degrees above absolute zero.

Peachy. Just what I needed! The rope above me started tugging, and I yelled to Dwayne to hold up a minute.

"Bill," I called, "you see that white rock just a few inches above your right hand? That's the rock I held onto. Can you reach it, Bill?"

He put his hand up and grabbed the rock; but he didn't pull himself up. He sank lower on his legs until his arm was stretched uselessly tight. My own arm ached, just watching.

"Bill, stand up! Just take a step higher, just one more step. There's a solid foothold just eighteen inches above your left foot. Plant your foot, lift your left hand, and step up on your left foot."

He looked up at me, and I stopped breathing. Bill was chanting something over and over. I couldn't hear it, but his lips looked like they were saying, "Every good boy does fine," the mnemonic we learned in music class to memorize the notes on the treble staff.

He cocked his head quizzically, waiting for me to answer an urgent question that no one could ask.

Then he simply let go of the cliff.

Quicker than thought, I flattened myself against the wall, bracing for impact. The rope jerked Bill to a halt; miraculously enough, it didn't break! I lost one foot and one hand—I felt my other foot slipping under Bill's dead weight. *"F-A-L-L-I-N-G!"* I shouted to warn Dwayne; I hoped he heard, because a second later, I was dangling straight off the rope myself.

We pendulumed back and forth, and I stared up at the ominous sight of the rope rasping back and forth against the rough stone. It wasn't a nylon line rated for thousands of pounds; it was glorified clothesline, never meant to hold the weight of two fully grown people!

Because the cliff sloped away from us, I had a hard time even touching it. I kept spinning around, dragged by Bill's own spinning . . . he wasn't even trying to catch hold again. Finally, by stretching my arm until I thought it would pop out of the socket, I managed to grab an outcropping with my fingertips and stop the lateral motion.

I kipped a couple of times, starting myself swaying back and forth slightly. At long last, on a forward swing, I caught a good grip and reeled myself in. I clawed for a foothold.

Then I had to do the hardest thing I'd ever done in my young life. I had to pull myself up a couple of steps, with Bill hanging off my waist—crushing my ribs and lungs, as advertised. I wasn't worried about the rope between me and Bill; it was the rope above my head I sweated . . . it had two hundred and fifty pounds hanging off it!

Straining until I thought my gut would explode, so great was the pressure, I managed one step, one more. My arms and legs felt like lead weights—I was supporting Bill all by myself! But when I looked up, a burst of adrenaline gave me new strength.

The rope above me was frayed and unraveling where it scraped the rock. It was going to snap the next time anyone put any pressure at all on it.

Naturally, panic-stricken Dwayne chose that moment to try to haul me up bodily with his enormous, brute muscle. He pulled until the rope was tight, then he yanked hard, twice.

On the second tug, the rope above my head snapped. It sounded exactly like when I break a handful of dry spaghetti noodles in half before dropping them in the boiling water.

Dwayne started shrieking like a maniac, bellowing,

"Jeannie! Are you all right? Jeannie, say something!" But I was too busy hugging the cliff, trying to hold up both myself and Bill by four tiny anchor points, two hands and two feet, none of them made of steel.

Without warning, the pressure below me dropped to nothing. Frantic, I looked down, certain that Bill had plunged to his death in the icy water below.

It wasn't that; Bill had suddenly awakened and found his own foot-and handholds. He looked up at me and raised his eyebrows. "You shouldn't have tried that," he said, shaking his head while chuckling sadly.

"Tried what?" I gasped, too zoned to pick up the warning signs: that was Beta-Bill speaking to me then.

"She who betrays the captain and leaves him alive . . . she understands nothing about Bill Hicks." It sounded like a line; I thought he might be quoting something, some movie; but I couldn't bring it out of the memory hole. In any case, I was too exhausted for stupid games and psychotic delusions of persecution.

"I didn't do anything!" I snapped, taut as the rope that had just split. "Are you all right? Can you make it?"

I looked up and realized my own position was more precarious than Bill's. I had shifted several feet to the right from where I had been. In my present spot, I had nowhere to go: a huge, vertical crack above me cut me off from my previous route. I would have to shift quite a bit farther to the right to find a way past it.

Without fear, totally subsumed by his delusional state, Bill calmly free-climbed up the face to a point even with my position. He stopped there, clinging to the cliff like a spider missing half its legs, and smiled like Huck Finn. "Let me help you," he said.

I recognized that look. It was the expression he always wore when he was lying through his teeth. I had no choice, however. Without Bill's help, my only option was to climb the crack above my head using a layback, a difficult climbing maneuver that I'd only watched, never done.

Bill, however, ten feet to my right, had fairly good climbing above him. If I could get level with Bill, I would be able to recover without plunging four stories down into the river.

Unfortunately, there were no holds in between us that I could see, not a single one.

"Bill," I said evenly, trying to keep the edge of panic out of my voice, "I'm going to climb down below you. Then you hang on tight—I mean really tight—and I'll swing on the rope until I'm right beneath you. Then I'll climb up and we'll continue on. Can you do that?"

"Of course," he said, still grinning. Still lying. But there was nothing else I could do.

I suddenly realized we'd left Dwayne totally hanging—literally. He was shouting himself hoarse up above, and I finally answered him.

"We're both still on the cliff, Dwayne!" I yelled. "The rope broke, but we haven't fallen!"

"I'm coming down!" he screamed.

"No! You'll kill yourself, trying to free-climb down a wet cliff backward! It's much better if you stay where you are. We'll come up. Then I'll tie the rope ends together . . . all right?"

"Well . . . I don't like it."

"And how many mountains have *you* climbed?"

He was silent for several beats. "Counting this one, one."

"Then do what I tell you. This is an emergency situation here! I don't have time to deal with everyone individually! *Stay in line!*" I don't know what I meant by that last sentence, but it always seemed to work for junior high teachers herding kids through the Model-Train Museum on a field trip. I thought it might be some sort of magical spell, like Dante's, "This has been willed where what is willed must be."

"Stay here?"

"Stay there! Stay where you are! Don't move until I find you!"

"All right," he said meekly. I barely heard him.

I turned to Bill again. "I'm starting now," I enunciated. "Just hold tight and don't move. I'll warn you before I hang on the rope."

I climbed slowly downward. Descending down a rock is truly a bitch, because you can't see where you're going. Particularly this time, since the overhang was sharpest at my location. I took it very, very slowly, not sparing Bill even a single glance.

I was trembling, and not just from the strain; I sweated, and my heart pounded—and not just from the exertion. My brain processed everything Bill had said and done since he dropped. I definitely knew which Bill I was dealing with. I was uncomfortably aware that until I got ahead of him again, I would be completely in Beta-Bill's power: he controlled the horizontal; he controlled the vertical.

I spotted a slight ridge. It wouldn't be enough to hold me by itself, but I could crawl along it if I hung off the rope. I would have to depend upon Bill.

I felt cold and clammy . . . and not just from encrusted sweat.

I stopped and looked up. "Okay, Bill. I'm ready to cross over now." I slowly increased the weight I put on the rope, praying—literally praying, to God Almighty—that it wouldn't snap.

I had just started to move when Bill spoke again for the first time since before I started my descent. "You shouldn't make me do this, Jet. I don't want to do it, but you made me."

I looked up, and my breath caught in my throat. Bill let go with one hand—God knew how he was hanging on, holding the both of us!—reached into his jacket and drew out a knife.

My knife!

I grabbed where it had been and found only my belt, nothing slipped inside. I stared at Bill in horror.

"I'm sorry, Jet," he said, "but we have to break up. You know how it is. Don't go away! I have to leave, Jet; I have to go away now. Don't cry, it's almost over."

Bill began to saw energetically at the rope.

Ten

"Bill . . . Bill, you don't need to do this! We can work it out—don't you remember all the times we had together?"

I was talking, but he wasn't listening. He was talking to the invisible person next to him. This was it, the confrontation with pure Beta-Bill . . . and I was about to become pure fish bait.

He was having some trouble with the rope, mostly because of the awkward angle. For a wild moment, I thought I might shimmy up the rope while he was sawing on it and karate-kick the knife out of his hand like the Ninja Turtles my brother Jaq is so fond of. Then I snapped back to reality.

I was still leaning one-half to three-quarters of my weight on the rope, and I couldn't get a good hold, no matter how frantically I clawed. But just two feet below me was a wide, flat ledge about two inches deep.

I turned my feet inward and hugged the face. Bill

finally got purchase enough on the rope and sliced through it—and I dropped like a proverbial R.

The natural impulse is to push away from the cliff, but that's exactly the wrong thing to do! I shoved every square inch of my body against it instead, and the face ripped me to shreds as I fell. I felt like I was being flayed alive!

My left foot missed the ledge, but my right landed solid. I dropped to a one-legged crouch, windmilling my arms to avoid tumbling backward three stories into the churning river.

I caught a precarious balance and leaned into the cliff; thank God it was not even quite straight up and down at the ledge, let alone concave, as it was higher up toward the bulge. I wanted to stand quickly, but my brain overrode my adrenal gland; I did a one-leg knee-bend, silently thanking Mother Dearest for forcing me to take two years of ballet when I was ten.

I gently probed the cliff, finally finding a pair of handholds; I got my left foot onto the ledge, and I was stable—more or less. More less than more, actually. I looked up.

Bill was staring down at me in annoyance. What's the matter with me? Why didn't I just drop off the cliff, like I was supposed to? "You're getting to be quite clingy, Jet."

"Yeah, well, since I'm still clinging to the mountain, I guess that's fair." I probably shouldn't have smart-mouthed him, but I had gone long beyond fear all the way to bitter anger.

"We have to break up. I can't carry you any longer, Yeoman Taylor. I know you're disappointed, but the good of the many outweighs the good of the few . . . or the one."

Either he had been reading the anti-individualist Jeremy Bentham—"the greatest happiness of the greatest number is the foundation of morals and legislation"—or else it was another *Star Trek* reference I didn't get.

Bill had my full attention; even the mountain I clung to was a distant second. I watched him intently as he began to climb spiderlike down the cliff. I'd never seen him so adept at finding the smallest crack or pebble to hold his weight. His fingers were as strong as a madman's . . . probably not surprising.

He *chuckled* as he climbed. That sent a shudder through me—of revulsion, not terror! The same feeling you get when you see a two-headed dog at a sideshow.

Bill descended slowly but steadily, and I had only a few seconds to figure out what the heck I was going to do about it. He wasn't climbing down to rescue me, or even apologize. His "unkindest cut of all" having failed to splatter me on the rocks below, the ghoul was coming to kill me more forthrightly.

How on earth had he gotten hold of my knife? He'd never been near me! I remembered putting my hand on it—I knew I had it then, unless we were all hallucinating—so when could he have possibly...?

Oh, man. I knew when he'd done it—it was when he pushed up against me and whispered in my ear his lies about Dwayne.

Jesus. He was—Jesus! Talk about cold . . . *the entire exchange was manufactured* just to give Bill an excuse to get close enough to lift my knife. The killer was slick. He was *slick!*

I edged along the ledge to my left, just trying to get out of his flight path; if he slipped—and he was climbing so fast!—I didn't want to be freight-trained down the hill. Besides, if I stayed stuck to the rock like Velcro, all he'd have to do is kick me in the face a few times and it'd be all adios, I'm a ghost.

He made it down to my level in record time. We clung to the side of the cliff, staring at each other across the gulf of sanity.

"This will hurt," he said. No smile; no emotion. Statement of fact.

"Somebody," I added.

With no more words, Bill Hicks crossed the line and came at me, knife again in hand. He had one thought.

I edged farther away, but it was a dweeb's game. He was faster on the hill, not worried about plunging to his death, and I was running out of ledge anyway.

"If you stab me," I warned, "the police will find the stab wounds and they'll know you did it. They'll put you away!"

It worked . . . sort of. He stopped, momentarily

pondering the situation. One of Bill's many books distinguished between serial and spree killers by the level of premeditation and preparedness. Spree killers generally just got a gun or a can of gasoline or something and started killing with no thought for getting away with it.

Serial killers, however, were more methodical. They prepared a place for the killing and lured the victim there; they even knew what they were going to do with the body before they even started.

The current situation had to be uncomfortable for Bill—he clearly fell into category two, not category one. He had planned this for some time—days. But he couldn't have made the kind of preparation he had made for the others he had already murdered, like...

"Is this how you got rid of Lalla?" I asked, trying to throw him off-balance. I couldn't quite keep a small note of panic out of my voice, and Bill heard it.

He slid the knife back into his tight belt, still staring at me. "Did you know you have a twin, Jet? She's just like you. She's just *exactly* like you. She even had the same flaws. She was imperfect. We had to split up."

I swallowed hard, noticing the sudden change of tense from present to past. See? Studying grammar has its uses.

Bill looked down the mountain, completely unconcerned about the drop, even about the water below, despite his phobia about water. Of course, that was Alpha-Bill's phobia; Beta-Bill had no fears.

Alpha-Bill was afraid of the world, but Beta-Bill wasn't afraid of anything. Gee, how subtle. I guess Beta had to kill anyone who had seen too much of Alpha, like pirates who killed the crewmen who helped them bury their treasure (and therefore knew where to find it later).

"It will be best if you just let yourself faint, Jet. You can do it. Otherwise, it'll hurt like a son of a bitch when you hit the rocks, which I don't think you can clear."

"They'll find you! They'll know you did it! You didn't prepare a place, didn't get everything all set . . . this is sloppy, totally outside the method!"

Bill shrugged. "I know, but there's not much chance of a conviction. I can say you just slipped." He mused again. "I'll have to take care of Dwayne too. He's seen too much interaction between us. But that part will be a pleasure."

I tried to think of something to say, but nothing came out of my mouth. I wasn't afraid, and I was about to tell Bill when it occurred to me that it might be my only advantage—*let him think it!* urged Miss Taylor; *let the monster think you're paralyzed with fear!*

"I've studied this, you know," Bill continued his lecture. "If you don't die in the fall—which is still possible, probably the best you can hope for—then your lungs fill with water in a few breaths. But you don't drown right away. It takes several minutes of oxygen deprivation before permanent brain damage sets in . . . usually around four minutes, but it varies from person to person."

He edged closer along the ledge, enjoying the performance, sucking energy from my fear. I was afraid; I won't lie; but a freaky kind of unreality settled over me . . . a movie, not real life.

At once I was like totally calm, *sang-froid*. I could have climbed the whole mountain just as Beta-Bill had, in a state of grace. I wondered if this was what that mountain climber felt when he unhooked his line a few years ago and free-climbed the face of Half Dome?

I turned my face away . . . it was the hardest thing I'd ever done. But I had to maintain the illusion of paralyzing terror.

I couldn't let Bill know I was waiting for him.

"This will hurt you more than it will hurt me," he explained unnecessarily.

I felt the living mountain beneath my fingers. Pressing my face against the rock, I felt every vibration as Bill Hicks slid closer. I was perfectly balanced. The earth moved through me—and a chorus of five hundred angels sang Bruckner in my head.

They reached the climax of his *Libera Me* just as the sound, the vibes, and my hypersensitive skin told me Bill stood next to me. His breath warmed the back of my neck, killing breath, the wind of God.

Bill reached out. I balanced on my left foot and raised my right slightly, desperately trying not to telegraph what was coming. *You only have to cripple him,* said Miss Taylor. *Just get his kneecap or his groin—you can outclimb him if he's injured!*

Yeah. Good advice. And maybe he'll grab the knife and stab me in the thigh.

I didn't want to think about it—but I knew what I had to do. Eat or be eaten.

I kicked backward with the strength of five hundred pushing my foot. Squeezing shut my eyes, I felt the shock up my leg as I connected; I felt a knife blow in my gut . . . but it was my innocence splitting me open, dripping down the mountain, not a real knife.

Clenching my teeth, I kicked again as Bruckner exploded inside me, drowning out Bill's startled gasp. The scrabbling sound as his feet slid from the ledge. The scrape as his hands clawed for a grip. The brass horns blew across his scream, a long, discordant note.

I pressed my face against the rock. The rock was wet; I wet it with my tears.

Bile rose up my throat, but I swallowed it down. I cried; I had never cried like that before, not even when my father . . . when we buried him.

Silence; the piece ended. I did not hear the splash. If he broke against the sharp stones below, I didn't hear that either. I heard my heart, the blood swooshing in my temples, the faint, musical chime of teardrops striking flint. I didn't hear his death scream.

Maybe he died on the rocks; but if he didn't, he died in the river . . . God knows I knew he couldn't swim.

He was always afraid of the water. I guess it wasn't a phobia after all.

The rock was colder than I thought it should be; maybe it was my skin. I was afraid to open my eyes: maybe Bill was still there, about to push me off with a laugh. I opened my eyes.

I was alone on the mountain. I'd done it. I killed Bill Hicks . . . and I didn't know what to do. I had half a mind to follow him . . . I didn't even know if I wanted to live.

Now I couldn't stop the explosion up my throat; I held the mountainside as tight as I could, letting it come, letting it fall. My stomach continued to heave long after it was empty of everything I'd ever eaten in my life.

I don't know how long I clung to the cold, cold cliff; long enough. I woke to hear Dwayne shouting, calling for me . . . was I all right? Was I still on the rock? Should he come down and get me? I'd heard it before.

I tried to answer, tell him God no, stay where he was, the last thing I wanted was . . .

But I was too scared. I started shaking, crying, making horrible animal noises, and I couldn't stop! My knees buckled—*Jesus, Jesus, what could I have*

*done? What else could I do? He came at me! He was
going to kill me!*

I didn't imagine it—*I didn't murder my friend!*

"I'm coming down!" hollered Dwayne, and at last I
found my voice.

"Don't come," I said, weak as a kitten.

"Are you all right? Jeannie, what's wrong?"

"Don't come! Stay—I'm coming up. I can come up
now. It's all right. . . ."

I guess it was all right enough. Dead inside, I crab-
walked along the ledge to the right, past where Bill
had been when he . . . when I . . .

I edged along to the vertical crack. I had never
done a real layback before. I decided this was the
trial: if I made it up the cliff, then God forgave me. If
not, I would join Bill forever in death, and that would
be my eternal damnation.

You lay back, like the name says, and put your
feet against the far side of the crack. You grip the
near end and use isometric pressure to keep your
feet planted. You shuffle upward, very slowly. It
takes strength and determination, maybe a little
insanity.

The mountain tried to throw me; the cliff tried to
crumble. The rain-slick stone tried to squirm under
my feet, but I beat them all.

The shale cracked, but I held my position. I
scrambled up twelve feet of layback in a state of
numb limbo.

I would have crawled even further, shimmied up

the split until my arms collapsed, dropping me right into Bill's waiting arms, if I hadn't felt a soft finger caress my face.

I blinked, focusing my eyes; it was the rope . . . the severed end that Bill had cut.

Transferring from a layback to the rope was a hell of a trick. The crack had widened as I climbed. By stretching my legs, I was able to press my back against the near edge and plant my toes like a ballerina against the far; once again, Mother Dearest is a fortune-teller.

A chimney! I could chimney; I'd done *that* before.

Cold as the grave, I tied the dangling end of the rope to the piece still circling my waist. I was connected again to Dwayne; but we had lost the weak link.

Next thing I realized, Dwayne was pulling me over the hump with his right hand. I don't remember climbing the last bit, but I must have. "We can't stop," I said. "Got to get higher, find the ledge. It's up here . . . it is! Climb!"

Dwayne's face was ashen, looking for the trailing rope and seeing nothing but a loose end. He turned away and started up the rock again.

We found the damned ledge about ten or fifteen feet higher. It was narrow, just a fault line where there'd been some geological movement. But we could sit, dangling our legs, and stare out over the still-flooded valley. We could talk, but we didn't. Didn't have anything to say.

"I don't want to take the lead," said Dwayne at last. His voice was husky with fear.

"We're not scaling any more cliff, Dwayne. The ledge is wide enough that we're going to follow it; from the ground, I saw that it cuts all the way across the face to the shoulder, and it's a shallow slope from there to the peak."

"Shallow?"

I smiled, grim and exhausted. "Well, comparatively speaking. Not a vertical adventure. It's steep, but you can hike it."

"Jeannie…"

"I'll tell you later."

"Is he…?"

"You see him sitting up here with us, big guy?" Jeez, I didn't mean it to sound so bitter. I wrapped my arms around my body, wishing someone would just hold me and tell me it was all right. Anybody—even Dwayne.

He stood. "Left or right?"

"Thataway."

With every step, I grew heavier and heavier, until I weighed nine hundred pounds. *No,* I thought, *it wasn't Bill; there was no Bill. There never had been any Bill!* He had been nothing but a little girl's dream a dozen years ago, and I had just awakened at last.

Yeah, that's it. Right. Dwayne slogged on ahead, not looking back. I doubt he could even face me. He didn't know what exactly happened; but he knew it wasn't simply a terrible accident, from my reaction if nothing else.

Did I really mean to kill him? I still didn't know. The whole adventure on the cliff was fogging over, like I was seeing all the different possibilities of what could have really happened all mushed together: Bill over here, over there, coming at me, coming to help me; Jeanette kicking her best friend off the mountain; Jeanette just trying to push him away with her foot. Jeanette being so freaking paranoid that she murders an innocent boy. Jeanette saving her miserable life by stealing another's.

There were two Jeanettes, really: the brain, who insisted that *he was going to kill me* and I had every right to defend my own life; and the heart, or I guess it would be the glands, which kept screaming *killer, killer, killer! Just like Bill!* I think I was turning schizophrenic for a while.

Then a miracle finally occurred; all my emotions finally overloaded and shut down entirely, and I became Jeanette the Android. I looked at the whole scene logically, and there was simply no question: I had just saved my life without any help from anybody. I should be proud.

If I'd had any emotions left, I suppose I would have been.

Dwayne and I didn't speak for the rest of the climb. If he had any private hells of his own, he didn't share them. I suppose he was mixed up himself; he

certainly had no reason to love Bill Hicks, but no
sane kid can feel real pleasure at another kid's death.
Even someone like Bill . . . even with what Dwayne
knew Bill had tried to do to me in the stick-castle.

Then I hit the downside of being an emotionless
creep: I started analyzing every tiny thing Bill had
said or done, finding a million different spins to put
on each word or lie that made it sound more innocent and innocuous and less like the ravings of a serial killer. God forgive me, I started trying to talk
myself into believing *I* was the murderer!

What now—did I have to shut down my *brain,*
too?

I struggled against the demon of doubt. It was self-
defense! I had to keep telling myself over and over. It
took me three hours before I finally believed me.

The understanding and self-forgiveness finally
came when we scrambled hand-over-hand up a final,
muddy promontory and found ourselves staring at a
weak, pathetic signal fire—and Neil and Samma.

Neil looked at me, and he didn't say anything for a
moment; he just looked. When he looked at me like
that, I fell to my knees, sobbing like a— Jeez, this is
stupid. I was about to say "sobbing like a girl." Okay,
sobbing like a *typical* girl.

But I wasn't crying out of pain or despair or even
joy at finding my soul-buddy. It was relief, totally.

I finally *knew,* deep in my brain and heart and
glands and everywhere else, that *I WAS RIGHT.* And
I wasn't a murderer. I wasn't Bill!

I looked up, more grateful to Neil than I'd ever been in my life. He gave me back my sense of who I was, just by being there and still being who *he* was.

And *then* we finally had our Goddamned joyous reunion. Sorry about the language.

Eleven

I ran over to Neil, noting *en passant* that his left leg was strapped into a makeshift splint. I dropped to the ground to hug the stuffing out of him. I held him, head buried in his shoulder, until my heart finally returned to normal and I stopped puffing like an overworked freight train. By then, Samma had shifted from patting me on the back to bodily prying me off her boyfriend.

She hugged me too, but it was halfhearted; and she pulled back and turned her face away. I notice things like that; I'm very sensitive to the moods of my friends, or at least I like to think so.

It was more than Samma's usual annoyance at the close friendship between me and Neil; this was something deeper. She and Neil must have been having their own interpersonal problems—hopefully not like me and Bill.

Ulp. . . . The time had come. Dwayne was squatting respectfully a few feet away, and Neil and

Samma had by now noticed that we were only four, not five. All eyes turned to me in expectation.

"He, um, well, just what you think happened."

Dwayne struggled. He wanted to say something, but something held him back . . . maybe he thought of himself as too much a gentleman. "Jeannie, how did Bill . . . fall?"

I said nothing. I mean, what was I supposed to say? That he was a homicidal maniac, and I kicked him off the cliff, and he fell onto the rocks or into the water and was swept away?

Yeah. That would go over like a lead balloon.

"I don't know exactly what happened. I know he fell, and I know he's . . . dead. But I don't know *why* everything happened the way it did."

It was a big mistake. I was always a rotten liar. Neil and Samma both stared at me, terrified of what they were thinking; and even Dwayne grimaced. I can't blame them; it sounded totally lame even to me.

"Jeannie," Dwayne persisted, "I don't want to keep poking at your pain, but . . . but I couldn't help notice this." He reached down and picked up the rope that was still tied around my middle. Two ends stuck off of it in opposite directions. One had led up to Dwayne, and that end was frayed, obviously torn apart by too much weight on the line.

The other end, the one that led down to Bill, was neatly knife-cut.

"Oh boy," I muttered. My explanation had just

gone from lame to what the police always call an inconsistent statement.

"You, ah, probably want me to explain why the rope was . . . why it looks like it was cut with a knife. Don't you?"

Neil smiled wanely. "It would help, Jet."

Samma just stared at the rope, then turned cold, suspicious eyes on *me,* on the person who was supposedly her best girlfriend. Dwayne scowled at the dirt.

"Bill cut the rope," I said with a tiny voice.

"Bill?" Skeptical Samma; thanks, girl.

"Bill cut the rope himself."

"He wanted to kill himself?"

"Samma . . . he wanted to kill *me.*"

She took a step back, eyes wide in surprise and incredulity. Dwayne looked up, face impassive. "Jeanette," said Samma, "I saw how you two were acting earlier; you really didn't like Bill, did you?"

"Easy, Samma," said my only quasi-defender, Neil. "I can vouch that Jet and I both loved Bill. He was our best friend!"

"When?"

"Well, we hadn't seen him in a long time. But there's no reason to think Jet had anything against Bill."

Dwayne looked at me, tight-lipped, his face turning a whiter shade of pale. He knew! Or at least, he had guessed.

I lowered my head, drawing a line on the ground

with my foot. I just couldn't do it . . . I couldn't put Dwayne in the position of having to lie for me out of some weird sense of chivalric honor.

"Yes there was," I said, my voice cracking.

"What? I couldn't hear you."

I looked my "best" girlfriend in the face. "I said I *did* have something against Bill, damn it! Dwayne can verify, he—he attacked me. Earlier."

"What do you mean, attacked?" She gasped as she figured out what I was dancing around saying. "Jesus! He did? He really did?"

I closed my eyes. I had no choice now; I had to spill everything. Well, almost everything. "He had kept touching me all through the hike. Then he . . . I built this house out of branches, you know? And we were going to sleep in it, you know? But then Bill asked Dwayne to go—to go outside, and he went, and that left Bill and me alone together, and I didn't th—think anything about it because we'd known each other for so long, and he hadn't ever . . . I mean, he did when we were kids, but that didn't mean anything!"

My cheeks were wet. When had I started crying again? Angry, I pushed on. "Then he . . . took off his clothes."

"God! Everything?"

"He took off his clothes, and he—he came at me…" I could hardly talk, trying to hold back sobs like I'd never felt before . . . but it wasn't because of his stupid attempt to do me . . . it was because of where this all was leading.

Somebody took my hand. It was Neil. He had sat up, and was stretching his hand as far as he could reach. I didn't move closer; I didn't want anyone touching me then. But I didn't drop his hand; I didn't want to hurt him.

"He came at—at me, and I got my camp—my camping knife out, and I held him off, and I got outside. And Dwayne came back . . . I think I screamed or something. And I couldn't tell him what happened, and I hid the knife b—behind my back . . . and . . . but I think he figured—figured it out—but he didn't s-say anything."

For a few seconds, I couldn't see or hear anything. Horrible pressure built up inside me, like a geyser about to explode. Then it faded, and I was dull, a pencil that wanted sharpening. "Bill was really onto me 'cause of it. He kept bagging and getting like real aggressive, you know? Like he kept touching me whenever Dwayne wasn't looking. And then he started talking crazy, saying I was doing what his old girlfriend Lalla did to him—and I think he killed her too—and he said he was going to do the same to me. And then he got his chance when we were on the mountain. The rope broke, and Bill and I were cut off from Dwayne... and then Bill cut the rope when I was hanging off of it, and he climbed down and came after me. And I..."

I opened my eyes. I had the undivided attention of the entire universe. "And he came at me."

"And?" prodded Dwayne.

"And I..."

"What did you do, Jeannie?"

"Don't call me that."

"Stop avoiding the question, Taylor," snapped Samma. "What did you do when he allegedly came at you?"

I looked at her ... and I've never felt such hatred before for another woman. "He *came at me!* And I kicked him. And he fell, the end." *End of relationship, Glynnis,* I thought, feeling nauseated. How could another girl say such a thing? How could she?

My face turned bright red ... not a good time for that reaction. It looked like I was feeling guilty ... and of course I was—all that work I'd done to convince myself I was right and he was wrong was thrown off the mountain by a single, stupid, insensitive comment from another girl.

But I *was* right; he *did* come at me! Damn it, damn it, *damn it,* there was nothing else I could do except stand there and be killed by that—that *monster.*

"This wasn't the first time he'd killed, you know!"

"Oh? He told you about it?"

"Not in so many words, but yes, he did!"

Neil interjected. "What did he say exactly, Jet? Near as you can remember."

"Exactly? I don't..."

"As near as you can remember. What exactly did Bill say?" Neil was swallowing over and over; I love him dearly, but he has a terrible tendency to mask his emotions by putting on his Mr. Spock face: he becomes totally logical, and you can't break through it.

"He said…we had to break up; that I was just like Lalla, like her twin; he said I was going to fall, and it would hurt, and I'd drown if I didn't die on the rocks. He said I had to…" I stopped. Suddenly, I was dizzy and sick, and I couldn't remember all he'd said. I wasn't taking notes, for heaven's sake!

I stared from Dwayne's pensive face to Samma's, and even my defender turned away and frowned. I don't know if he didn't believe me either or he was just dealing with his oldest, best friend suddenly dead at the bottom of a cliff, and his other best friend having killed him and saying he was a rapist and a killer.

I didn't blame Neil or Dwayne. I don't think I would have believed me either, if I weren't there and didn't see it. Samma no longer existed, as far as I was concerned.

"What happened to the knife?" asked Dwayne, perplexed.

"I don't have it. Bill had it. He cut the rope, then he put the knife in his belt. See? I don't have it any-more."

No one said anything; they were too polite. But of course, I realized as soon as I said it that it didn't prove a thing. I could have dropped it myself as soon as I finished cutting Bill loose to fall to his death.

A long, long, awkward silence. Nothing to say. I couldn't even think of any poetry. My brain was dead.

"So," said Dwayne, in a changing-the-subject tone, "what happened to you guys?"

Neil rushed through the open door. "We weren't washed very far by the floodwaters. I got snagged on a tree root—that's how I got this beauty." He indicated his leg. Now that I looked, I saw it was a bad break. The shin bulged ominously under a heavy wrap of Ace bandage; but I didn't know enough medicine to tell whether it was just radical swelling—which could be a serious infection—or if it was a compound fracture, poking up through the flesh.

Either way was horrifying. We tend to forget that infection still kills millions of people every year, worldwide. And being in the wilderness was the same, whether you were in the U.S. or a Third World nation. No doctor; no antibiotics; no medicine.

Not even any painkillers . . . and it must have hurt like anything. I had a sudden, new respect for Neil Armstrong; he was awesome about not showing his pain . . . since we couldn't do anything about it anyway.

"We climbed out of the river . . . well, actually, Samma climbed out and dragged me onto the mudbank. Then she splinted my leg. God, she's a great nurse; I think she's planning to be one when she gets to college."

"Or a doctor, like as not," she said, pro forma.

Neil winced; a sudden shot of pain. Then he continued as if nothing had happened. "Not much else to tell. We figured we'd head for the Hag's Tooth . . . tallest mountain for miles around. Figured you'd come here, eventually, if you—if you made it."

Neil looked at me. I knew what he meant by his last caveat: he'd been terrified I was dead; and if I were, he might not be able to go on. I knew the feeling well.

I realized another thing: *Neil believed me.* Dwayne was unsure and Samma downright hostile . . . but why? Why was self-defense so impossible a thought to them?

I twitched my lips in an almost-smile at Neil, trying to tell him how grateful I was without drawing fire from his significant other.

I asked the question on both Dwayne's and my mind: "How'd you climb the cliff with your leg so banged up?"

"Cliff? What cliff?"

"Up the Hag's Tooth! We went from the west face, south along the hill, all the way to the east face—it was cliffs, cliffs, cliffs all the way!"

Neil stared at me for an instant. "You should have continued around to the north . . . you could have walked up the trail." He started to laugh, abruptly cutting it off when he realized that that one unlucky (or stupid) decision had cost Bill Hicks his life.

I covered my face with my hands, breathing slowly and deeply. All we had to do was walk a few more miles! The whole . . . the whole thing could have been avoided!

But we didn't. And it wasn't. Bill was dead, floating down the river, skin blue, eyes wide open and staring at the sky he couldn't see. And it was all my fault. I didn't remember the geography right.

Dwayne rumbled in the background, "We didn't know . . . we didn't have a map or anything. How were we supposed to know?" He meant how was *I* supposed to know—but I should have. I was the captain. It was my responsibility to know, or at least to check.

But at some level I knew it wouldn't have made any difference. Bill was on a hair-trigger, just waiting for his chance to pop. We never would have made it that far; the monster would have seen to that.

I folded my arms, feeling the same spirit possess me that allowed me to lead the boys as far as I had. "So what now, Neil? You seen any planes?"

He nodded. "They're out there. They know we're missing by now; and since they didn't find us where we were supposed to be, they've kind of figured we got caught in the flood somehow. Saw a pair of search planes just yesterday; we stoked the fire, but they didn't look this way. And I heard a helicopter last night, far away, but we didn't see anything. By the time we could get some wood on the fire and get it up, the noise was gone."

"But they are searching out this way, at least," I summarized.

"Just starting. We've got a chance." He grimaced again, sucking in a breath through tight teeth and gently holding his leg. The spasm lasted longer than last time.

"You look low on wood."

"That's why we're burning just enough to keep the fire going. Samma could only get one of her SuperMatches to work; if the fire dies out—it's gone."

"I thought those things lit anywhere," I grumbled.

"Well, evidently a flash flood voids the warranty. Anyway, she's only got one left, and we don't know if it's a working SuperMatch or another nonstarter."

"I can take care of the wood," volunteered Dwayne, grateful to find something he could do to help.

"When you get back," interjected Samma, "see if you can put together a set of crutches. We'll have to move, and we can't carry Neil. It was sheer hell getting him up here, and the leg is worse now."

"Halfway done." Dwayne wandered north, heading down toward the tree line.

"Samma hasn't wanted to leave me," said Neil, "not even to get more wood."

"Right, and come back and find you bled to death! Chance of that is dot."

All right, I decided, *I'd better build bridges instead*

of fences. I had plenty of time to ignore Samma for the rest of my life after we got back safely. "She was exactly right, Neil. Sticking with you to make sure you don't kick off is more important than gathering wood, especially now that Dwayne and I can do that stuff."

Samma looked away from me; she looked at Neil, but I knew she was just avoiding me. Well, fine; I didn't particularly want to be friends anyway, so long as we weren't enemies.

"Second question," I continued; "what do you have in the way of food, and more important, water?"

Neil licked his lips; he was hungry. "We . . . through some weird, administrative oversight, we seem to have ended up with most of the food." The administrative oversight was that the night before the flood struck, Neil rearranged all our packs— shifting all the food to his and Samma's! It was just bad luck, of course; he had no way of knowing the Vincent Hidalgo Dam would burst the next day, washing us all in separate directions.

"What's left?"

"Not much. Well, nothing, actually. Most of it was soaked in the flood, and it—it all rotted, Jet. I'm sorry."

"My freeze-dried food? It's all *rotted?*"

"Those bags aren't meant to travel through a raging river, girl-thing! They leaked, and the food expanded and burst the bags."

"Well, we can help y'all out on the food front," I said

cryptically. I slung my backpack on the ground—
Dwayne had already dropped his—and rummaged
through looking for a few ripe-smelling hunks of fric-
asseed Smokie the Bear.

Neil looked dubious. "Ah, what's this, Jet?"

"Just eat it and don't ask questions."

"It smells funny," declared Samma, still in no
mood to be charitable.

"Then eat a snail."

I wished I hadn't said it; I expected an explosion,
but Samma surprised me with a simple grunt. They
both fell ravenously upon the flesh of ursus, and
there was much gnashing of teeth. I must have
been feeling a bit better, for I couldn't help but
quote Milton:

"Blind mouths! . . .
The hungry sheep look up, and are not fed."

I had no idea what it meant, but it seemed appro-
priate somehow. They were the only lines of all the
lines and poems of John Milton I read that I still
remembered.

"Shakespeare?" guessed Neil; he knew as much
about English lit as I knew about rocket engines.

"The other guy."

"Milton?"

"How about water?"

"Counting the canteen and a half you brought?"

"Yes."

"A canteen and a half."

I stared. "You cannot be serious."

"All right, maybe two canteens. We're almost out. But we passed a small rivulet on the way up that was still dripping rain runoff . . . not for long, though; it hasn't rained up here in a couple of days. It might be dry already."

"Tell me where."

I found the spot, but the waterflow was reduced to a steady drop. I stuck a half-full canteen under it anyway, with a strip of cloth wrapped around the top to filter out sediment. In half a day, it might fill the canteen. In a survival situation, it's a sin to waste even a drop of potable water.

I returned, still suspect, to the hostile glare of Samma, the guarded, speculative examination of Neil Armstrong, and the depressed, tired need of Dwayne.

Here we were, the Four Musketeers. What next?

I thought of the Donner Party and shuddered.

Twelve

Night fell with a crash like a suit of armor falling over. Distant thunder . . . lightning but so far no rain. It was a mixed blessing; we wouldn't be soaked, but we wouldn't get any more water, either.

I remembered something I'd seen on a TV show once. I took Samma's empty water bottle, wrapped Dwayne's T-shirt around it—I swear I didn't even glance at his naked chest!—and buried the covered bottle in the mud, neck up. We'd see what we found come morning.

Dwayne had brought us back plenty of wood, so we sacrificed Samma's last remaining SuperMatch Fire Starter; it worked, a miracle! We stoked up a raging signal fire. Dwayne gloomed and stomped around, bagging on everybody and everything in sight. I thought maybe it was still the aftereffects of his dysentery; but Neil whispered that it sounded darker than that.

"I think he's getting close to total despair, Jet," he warned. We sat very close; Samma had been sitting on Neil's other side, but she angrily jumped up and walked around the other side of the fire, plopping down next to Dwayne and trying to rouse him into conversation about Australia. I didn't know what her problem was; Neil and I had been buddies since long before she ever landed in San Glendora.

"What's the next phase? Does he fling himself off the cliff?"

Neil looked at me strangely, and I flushed guiltily. What a crappy choice of words.

"I don't think he's suicidal, Jet Stream. I think the next stage is apathy . . . he'll just sit there and won't budge. He might not even eat. My…"

Neil paused, hurting inside. I put my hand on his. "What is it, Leap?"

"My mother went through a depression that turned into total apathy. Almost a year long."

"How'd you get her out?"

"Antidepressant drugs prescribed by a shrink."

"You, ah, didn't happen to bring any along?"

"Of course not. And he shouldn't take them, anyway."

"Why not? If it's an emergency—"

"Maybe it's no big deal taking Seldane or asthma medicine prescribed for someone else—but antipsychotics are totally different. You could like totally flip. I heard about a kid over at Warren G. Harding

High who took his father's Prozac 'cause someone told him it would cure insomnia."

"So what's the punch line?"

"So he freaked, and got a rifle, and shot his mother."

"Yeah," I said, a bit too sarcastically, "and this one girl murdered her entire family under the influence of marijuana. I saw *Reefer Madness* too, Neil."

He grinned. "All right, maybe it's an urban legend. But it's still a good point. The brain plays funny tricks . . . really strange. Everything you see is really inside your own head, you know?"

"Going to major in philosophy when you get to Berkeley, Leap?"

He turned to me and spoke with a peculiar intensity. "Under the stress of the moment, the brain can see things that just aren't there. It's not your fault, and it doesn't mean you're going crazy."

"Are we talking about Dwayne's depression—or are we talking about someone else? Me, for instance?"

Neil looked away and spoke very, very quietly. I could barely hear him, and Samma and Dwayne were totally out of earshot, even if Samma did stop talking herself. "I'm talking about panic. I'm talking about a guy dragging you down, maybe a guy hanging on his rope and pulling you off the mountain."

"Maybe you shouldn't talk about stuff you weren't there to see."

"My leg feels better; I feel like a short walk. Come

here for a second." We rose, and Neil and his miracle crutches led me out of the firelight, away from the other two. The sticks of wood actually worked; Neil could get around on them for a few minutes . . . then his leg started to throb, and he had to sit down. The swelling looked smaller, but I still couldn't tell if it was a compound fracture. And I wasn't about to ask Samma.

Neil spoke intensely, like someone trying to secretly coach a witness. "If he were off the rock and dangling from your rope, no one could blame you for cutting him loose. It was you or him, Jet . . . if that's what happened."

"You think I'd do such a despicable, cowardly thing, Neil?" I couldn't keep the bitterness out of my voice, and Neil flinched as if I'd actually hit him.

"I'm only saying it wouldn't be your fault. It would be an excusable homicide, I think the cops would call it. That would be the end of it. If—if that's the way it happened, I mean."

"I told you how it happened, Neil." An alien thought took root in my brain: *Take it, take the life-line!* it screamed. *He's letting you off, telling you what you need to say to get them off your back. You'll be free!*

Yeah. Free . . . and hated and despised as a craven jellyfish for the rest of my life.

Heck, I'd rather be in jail with my self-respect intact. It was weird, but I knew with utter certainty that I'd even rather people thought I was a murderer than a spineless worm "who in a perilous emer-

gency thinks with her legs," to slightly paraphrase
Ambrose Bierce.

"That's not how it happened, Neil. It happened like I
told you. Bill tried to kill me; I just got him first, somehow. I didn't mean to kick him off the mountain . . . but
I won't pretend to be grief-stricken."

Neil nodded and said nothing more about it. But I
couldn't let it just lie there. "I remembered something, Leap; you should remember this too. We all
went on an adventure down to Edwards Air Force
Base, that last summer before Bill moved."

"Yeah," he recalled, "to see the first Shuttle landing after they started up the program again. My dad
got us seats in the VIP section. We were supposed to
meet Bush, but all the government officials were too
chicken to show up, just in case it crashed."

"My brother, Jason, drove us. He was home from
UC Santa Cruz, about six months before—he died.
Remember what happened? On the trip, I mean."

Neil scowled; I knew that face . . . the elusive
memory hovered on the tip of his forebrain, but he
couldn't quite pull it loose. He knew it was important;
I would never have brought up my half-brother otherwise. I had never actually told him how Jason and
my dad died . . . someday I would have to. Mom
never talked about it because then she would have to
acknowledge that Jason existed, which meant admit-
ting Dad's double life.

"On the way down," I prompted, "we stopped at
Vandenburg for a tour of SLC-6, that was supposed to

be a Shuttle launch site until they killed it. The base Commanding Officer took us up to the top of the VAB, where we could look down and see all the cranes and stuff where they would have assembled the Shuttle and external tank. Do you remember when we were leaning over the railing and staring straight down about twenty stories?"

Neil's face turned white. He started to remember.

I was relentless. All I had left in the wasteland was my honor. "Bill suddenly told us to hold his feet. Then he leaned way, way over the railing—and he let go! If we had let go of his legs, he'd have dropped two-hundred feet and splattered against the concrete floor."

Neil nodded, lips pressed tight. "I remember being really grateful the brigadier general didn't see us. That would have ended the tour right then and there."

"Do you remember what Bill said when we hauled him up?" Neil didn't respond; he remembered, but he was being deep and cryptic.

The words were etched in my mind as clear as the hour Bill said them. He said, "I wish the whole world were hanging, so I could drop it." He said it with such pure, evil conviction that I shuddered.

Neil nodded. I didn't need to remind him. "We were only kids, Jet. How were we to know?"

As we returned to the fire, Neil hobbling and me with leaden feet, I knew I finally had one ally who loved me enough to believe me.

If I gained an ally, I also gained an enemy. Samma

was silently, sullenly glaring at us when we stepped
back into the light. Too late, I realized she might
think we were off fooling around—kind of a goofy
thing for her to worry about, with all that had happened; but that's Samma all over.

"I'll, ah, see you in the Viper Room, Leap." Neil
didn't respond . . . he was lost in a deep pool of
thought, too intent even to remember to sit, and that
was Neil all over.

I journeyed all the way around the fire and sat
next to Dwayne; I figured it was politic. Samma circled the fire with me, but on the opposite side, ending up next to her main dude. I wasn't quite sure
whether that meant we had circled each other; I
never understood that puzzle.

Dwayne drew doodles in the dirt with a stick and
periodically poked the fire. "So Dwayne," I said,
"what's the first thing you're going to do when we
get back?"

"Back?"

"Yeah. You know. Back?"

He shrugged. "Tell my parents, I guess."

I sighed. "Don't you think they'll already be told
by the cops? I mean, what's the first thing *you'll* do?
Get a pizza? Kick a field goal? Go to a movie?"

"I, uh, I've been thinking about Bill. What happened. I mean what happened with you in the hut."

I didn't exactly want to be reminded; but at least
he was talking, not just grunting. "Any great
thoughts?"

"I can see how that would be really horrible. Having him try to…molest you like that."

"Rape, Dwayne. The word is *rape*. Molesting is more like just touching, and Bill was going for the whole nine yards."

"Okay. I've been thinking that if I were a girl, that would be about the most horrible thing that could happen to me . . . I mean if it had gone all the way."

"You can't say it, can you?"

Dwayne's face darkened in the firelight. "If he had actually gone all the way and raped you." I said nothing; I had nothing to say. I didn't like the entire conversation, but I didn't want to stop him. "I think if that had happened to me, if there was maybe more than you said . . . maybe it went a little farther before you got away. I think if that happened to me, I'd be really full of anger and rage and stuff. I'd be totally flipping out."

"Yeah…?"

"I think maybe I'd be so insane, I might—you know."

"Do something to him?"

"Maybe."

"Push him off a mountain, maybe?"

"I'm not saying you did. I'm just saying I might understand a person who did that. It's like temporary insanity . . . a person could probably get off for inflammatory manslaughter."

I sat silent for a moment, swallowing my fury—at Dwayne, not Bill. "What TV show were you watching where they talked about that?"

He squirmed a bit. *"Matlock.* Why?"

"You watch *Matlock?"*

He turned darker. "My grandpa watches! He was just over at our house, and I was bored with trigonometry."

I took a deep breath. "Dwayne, in the first place, I think you mean involuntary manslaughter, not inflammatory. And that's not the same as temporary insanity, anyway. And third, *that's not what happened.* It happened just like I said: I'm not a liar, Mr. Cors. It was justifiable homicide—he came at me and tried to kill me, and all I did was defend my own life!"

Silence. Then Dwayne spoke in a huffy, offended voice. "I was only trying to help."

"That isn't helping. You could help me by believing me. The police need to believe me; but it's almost as important that my friends believe me—and you guys have more reason to, because you know me! You know I wouldn't kill a guy because I was stressed or temporarily insane or having a bad PMS day or anything like that! And I hate you all for even saying it."

I got up and walked away, alone into the darkness.

All right, maybe I overreacted. But if my *friends* wouldn't even believe me, what chance did I have with the cops?

Would even Mother Dearest believe me?

Then I was blinking back tears again; but this time, I wasn't going to let anybody see. I would come back to the fire when I was the captain again.

Neil still had his Walkman, and he claimed that sometimes he could hear broadcasts, even though all I heard was static when I listened. If there were a way to rebuild the thing to broadcast a help message, none of us had the faintest idea how.

But Neil came up with another signal: He made Dwayne stand up with Samma and one of my trash-bag parkas, holding it to cover the fire; then they dropped the bag and raised it again. I watched them from a distance, not yet ready to rejoin the mob.

Anyone watching from the direction where we were supposed to be would (possibly) see the signal fire blink.

They did this in the standard Morse code for rescue, SOS (save our souls): • • • — — — • • • If our luckstone were working, maybe someone would see the signal and figure it out. If someone who had a radio saw it, he could radio somebody else off a distance, and between the two of them, they could triangulate and figure out we were on top of the Hag's Tooth.

Yeah, and I could win the Lotto. Wish for the moon, girl!

When Dwayne and Samma got tired of flashing, they lay down to sleep. We left the signal fire burning; I set my watch alarm to get me up in time to feed the fire some more wood.

I was going to stay where I was; but it was cold as the ninth circle of Dante's *Inferno* up on that mountain. I reluctantly returned to the fire.

I lay next to Neil, on the other side from Samma. "Leap—it really means a lot to me that you believe me," I said.

I was working my way around to apologizing for being pissed earlier, but he disarmed me and left me speechless when he said, "If love means anything, it means you have to believe the girl you—you care for."

"But why? What made you decide to believe me?"

"Hmph. No logical reason, Jet. I didn't sit down and weigh everything out. I decided to believe you years ago; I'm just being consistent today."

"I'll put up with a lot, Neil Armstrong. But I demand *total loyalty* from my friends. Always remember that; I won't tell you again."

"I won't forget."

From the other side of Neil, Samma, who still didn't realize I wasn't speaking to her—maybe I was being *too* subtle— interrupted. "I don't know about you two lovebirds, but there's one Jillaroo who's dog-tired. How about we give it a rest, 'ay?"

The words were innocent enough; but the tone was bitter. I sighed; Samma was jealous again. She certainly had nothing to fear from me! My feelings for Neil were totally . . . they were like completely . . .

Were they?

Yes, I'm sure they were totally. Well, not *sure*-sure, not like I was sure about Neil's loyalty. But reasonably—

All at once, I wasn't sure of anything anymore. All

through this horrible adventure, I had been worrying about Neil, thinking about Neil, frightened half to death about what poker-hand fate had dealt to Neil. When I saw him alive again, it was like when Eurydice and Orpheus were reunited in the Underworld!

I thought for about a thousand years about our embrace. Now that I looked more objectively, I didn't think it was entirely platonic. In fact, you know, I kind of melted into Neil's arms, my body fusing with his in a way I'd never done before . . . except maybe in the occasional dream that I chalked up to dreamscape psychology and hormones.

My God. I think I kind of *liked* being touched by Neil Armstrong.

I cradled my chin on my wrists, staring at the fire. I didn't want these feelings . . . I wasn't really ready for them. Not for Neil. He was a nice guy—all right, he was the world's most wonderful guy. But he was a friend! I cringed at the thought of dating a friend.

So what would you rather date? Enemies?

No, Miss Taylor. Not enemies; just that there are two kinds of guys: friend-guys and date-guys. If I've already put a person in the first category, it makes me feel creepy to move him over to the second. Jeez, I still remembered Neil as a six-year-old boy . . . back when I was a six-year-old girl.

The boy next door . . . what a cliché! It was too stupid for words. No, I refused to be in love with Neil; it was just too weird.

I could swear it was unrelated, but I knew that

Neil and Samma's relationship wasn't long for the world. He wasn't her Mr. Right; he was Mr. Right Now. She really needed a strong, brave, macho Neanderthal, someone to get her Australian juices bubbling. She didn't want the sensitive, brainy type; she wanted Sylvester Stallone, except taller. And Neil didn't want someone who was always challenging him to be more like a cowboy; he didn't want to be a cowboy. He wanted a girl like—

Oh damn, there I went again. How much of my supposed "feelings" for Neil were real, and how much were just a reflection of the fact that he was the only one of the three to really believe I wasn't a murderess and a liaress?

"Jet," he whispered. "You asleep?"

"If I were," I pointed out logically, "whispering in my ear would probably have awakened me."

"Sorry. There's something I never told you about. Something between Bill and me."

"Big or small?"

"Horrible. Something so disturbing I never forgot it."

"Why didn't you ever tell me?"

He was silent a long time, and I started to worry that he'd fallen asleep. Then he finally answered. "Because I was so ashamed of it."

I realized I was holding Neil's hand. I couldn't remember having taken it.

"It was a few months before he moved. I was eleven and Bill was twelve."

"What about me?"

"You were at the doctor's. I think you had a rash ."

"Oh, like, thanks for reminding me!" What an insensitive dork. What a Neil Armstrong. I smiled, face red and warm.

"Bill asked me over to 'play doctor,' and I was half-ready to bolt if he took his clothes off or anything. But he was just joking . . . except he wasn't."

"Run that by me in slo-mo?"

"I mean he didn't mean play doctor like taking off your clothes or anything. He meant…Jesus, this is hard."

I waited, heart pounding. What was Neil about to confess to me? Some drug thing? Some gay thing? Something told me I didn't want to hear it, whatever it was. But he had listened to me and believed me; I was hono-bound.

"He had some puppies," said Neil. "Probably from Larceny."

"Larceny was a he. You can tell by—"

"Don't be a smart-ass. They could still be from Larceny, and you know it. We went out in the back-yard, and he brought one of the puppies with him. We played with it for a little bit, then . . . then he said he was going to show me what a real doctor did. He kept saying he was going to be a doctor, and it would be all right."

I looked past Neil and realized that Samma was staring at us, huddled together and whispering like schoolchildren in love. When she saw me looking at her, my former best girlfriend angrily rolled over, turning her back to us, and stared at Dwayne, who snored like a band saw.

Neil didn't notice—more evidence, if I needed it, that he and Samma were simply incompatible.

"He . . . he. . . ." Neil seemed to have trouble starting up again. "He had a bottle with him, unlabeled. Some kind of general anesthetic. He soaked a cloth with it, holding it downwind, while I held the puppy. I wasn't . . . *sure* what he was going to do, but my God, Jet, I had a pretty good idea. And I d-didn't do anything to stop him. Nothing!"

"Like you said to me, Leap: you were just a kid."

He closed his eyes, enunciating slowly. "Jeanette, I have to think I'm not the same as Bill Hicks. I have to! But how can I?"

I squeezed his hand tight. To hell with Samma Glynnis! Neil needed me right then and there. I'd deal with his paranoid girlfriend later.

"He put it to sleep, but he didn't kill it. Not then. He cut the p-p-poor thing open, and he—" Neil crushed my hand so hard, I thought I felt bones crack. *Thank God it wasn't Dwayne,* was all I could think for a moment, I mean aside from *aaaaaag!* "He did a really gentle exploratory surgery, slicing open everything and showing me all the insides.

"God help me, Jet—I watched. I felt sick; I was terrified that someone would come charging out and catch us. But I watched! I couldn't take my eyes off the mess. It was like I was paralyzed by the Gorgon, turned into a stone statue with no willpower to look away.

"Sometime during the scene, the surgery turned into an autopsy. I mean the puppy died, but Bill kept right on. He had a solid grasp of anatomy; he knew what everything was, the way you can only get by practical experience, not from a book."

"Leap, you weren't enjoying it. You were frozen in fear and revulsion. Nothing to be ashamed of."

"But I watched and learned. In high school, when we dissected the rat, I used that experience to get an A."

"You always got an A on anything scientific, Neil."

He lowered his head until it was resting in the dirt. "Don't you see, Jet? We *enabled* Bill. We're partially to blame for whatever he became—some kind of killer. He killed that girl, his old girlfriend; he would have killed you, and he would do it with the same unreal detachment that I saw when he dissected the puppy.

"He's our child, Jet. He was our child."

I wanted to tell Neil he was full of shit. I wanted to say that no one's to blame for a guy's crimes but the guy himself, the perpetrator. But I couldn't; the words stuck in my throat. Because I knew *I* was the one full of it . . . *somebody* made Bill. His parents shared some of the blame, didn't they?

And if his parents . . . why not his friends, the people he cared most about? The ones who *could have stopped him* before he moved away and murdered Lalla?

I lay quietly beside the low-burning fire, holding Neil's hand tight against my breast, trying to sleep when I knew I'd never sleep again.

Thirteen

I slept right through my watch alarm, if it even went off. Maybe the water killed it. All I know is when I bolted awake, the first rays of dawn pounded me in the face like a chalking mallet, and the fire was out, leaving only smoldering embers.

Only you can preserve forest fires! shouted Miss Taylor, as I hastily fed branches and leaves and other rubbish into the embers, coaxing them awake again. Neil and Samma blinked back to consciousness about the time I got a rosy blaze fired up. Dwayne was dead to the world.

At length the morn and cold indifference came.

Nick Rowe couldn't have phrased it better. Neil didn't talk; his leg was in too much pain, having stiffened in the night. Samma didn't talk; she was too much of a witch with a capital B. Dwayne didn't talk in his sleep. And I gazed into the middle distance, hoping to spot a bird, a plane, a frog, or even Underdog to come rescue us. We had a great signal fire—now whom could we signal?

I retrieved the two water bottles; the canteen under the dripping stream was only half full, but the one I buried was full—of dirty brown water. It was potable; you could drink it without getting sick.

Half-an-hour crawled past like this until finally Neil broke the ice. While Samma massaged his leg, gently feeling the break while he winced, Neil thought of subjects and chatted about them, undeterred by the fact that he was doing a solo act.

When he got around to "How 'bout them Giants?" I decided it was time to take charge.

"Somebody's going to have to go for help, Neil."

"It speaks. Tell me, O great Sphinx, how you plan to get across Sutter Stream flood plain, which probably has about three feet of mud in the lowest part?"

"I was thinking of Dwayne. He's the strongest; maybe he could push his way through."

Samma looked sharply at me. "Dwayne? Or maybe *me* and Dwayne? Is that about it, chum?"

"Look, Samma, first, get paranoid on your own time! We've got a situation here, and we need everybody. Even you. Second, I'm not speaking to you. Got it? And it has nothing to do with Neil or Dwayne or Bill or Hillary. This is between you and me—it's about a person who won't even believe her best girlfriend isn't a liar and a murderer!"

"Oh, and you expect me to believe you did a

karate kick on the cliffside, kicked the knife out of Bill's hand, then popped him off like Jean-Claude Van Damme; that's about it, eh matey?"

"What are you saying? You *are* saying I'm a liar!"

Samma jumped up, her face even more florid than normal . . . almost as red as the color she dyed her hair. "I didn't say that—but now I will. Yes, *I think you killed Bill Hicks.* And you snuffed him because it's *you* who's the psycho, not Bill! Bill was a perfect gentleman, and more of a man than your *boyfriend* here! And he kissed better than Neil, too!"

Neil said nothing; but his face first turned pale, then reddened around the ears and cheeks. He was worse than humiliated; he was practically destroyed.

He turned coldly to Samma. "I think you've said enough."

"I've not said nearly so much!"

"You've said enough!"

The bellow caught us all by surprise. I didn't even know Neil was capable of it. Dwayne had sat up when Samma first began to shout; now he stared back and forth like he was watching a three-way tennis match. He looked frightened.

Samma sat down. Then she stood up Then she sat down again. But it was a full minute before she spoke. She stood and folded her arms. "I'm not the only one, Taylor. Ask Neil. If he's an honest, decent man, as he claims to be, he'll cover my bet."

Neil glared at her with a cold eye. I shuddered at the look of it; if there'd been any doubt, the relationship

was now over . . . forever. "No, Samma. I think she
didn't do it. I think it happened just the way she said it
did . . . that's what I think. And that's as honest as I can
get."

She looked at him as if he had betrayed his country . . . and as if she had expected no better from him.
"Well, Dwayne; I guess it's up to you. Jeanette can't
vote; she's the accused. I say she's guilty of murder.
Neil—" Samma curled her lip in disgust, looking
down at her ex-lover, who still sat on the ground
holding his leg—"wants to believe she's pure as the
driven snow. She's Waltzing Mathilda. So what do
you say, Jackaroo?"

Dwayne stood, my jacket wrapped around him
like a blanket, which is how he'd been using it during
the night. "I'm . . . not voting."

"What happens if you vote against me?" I asked.

"No options, Taylor. We tie your hands and feet. You
could do any one of us in the night. Or you could run.
We can't take that chance. Consider it a citizen's arrest."

"And if the vote goes against *you?*"

She glared at me silently. When she spoke, it was
to Dwayne again. "No abstentions, Dwayne. House
rules: everybody votes except Jeanette."

"Just leave me out of it! Can't you people just get
along?"

"Can't we all just get along?" mocked Samma with
a really ugly—and I think racist—impersonation of
Rodney King. "Sorry, lad—no justice, no peace!" She
was in a real white-sheet-and-hood mood today. Any

minute now, she'd start burning crosses on the mountain peak.

Come to think of it, maybe that wouldn't be such a bad idea. It should certainly attract attention. The ACLU would find us in ten minutes.

Dwayne shook his head and turned away; but Samma wouldn't let him wriggle off the hook. "We need you, Dwayne; we need you to break the tie. It's one to one, and you're the deciding vote. So *bloody vote,* damn you!"

Like an automaton, Dwayne turned back to face her. "Don't make me do this, Samma. I don't— I'm just a friend! I only met you a few days ago, really met you. I don't even know Jeanette that well! Don't- don't make me do this!"

In the tight emotions of the moment, holding my breath—I swore out loud that I would abide by the group's decision, even if that meant being hog-tied until . . . *if* we were rescued—I almost missed the fact that under stress, Dwayne got my name right.

That bastard. He'd been doing that "Jeannie" stuff on purpose!

Samma riveted him to the deck with her eyes. *Say it,* her eyes demanded; *back me up. Tell me you don't believe her, and I'll make it worth your while.*

Dwayne looked down at the fire. "I believe her," he whispered.

"What?" asked Samma, incredulous, thinking she hadn't heard right. I let out a breath I hadn't realized I was holding.

"She's telling the truth. It was self-defense."

Neil looked at the woman who once was his. "Two to one, Samma. Majority rules. This is still America."

She turned her back on all of us. "Stupid country," she mumbled.

"Majority sides with Jeanette Taylor," said Neil, smiling once again. "The court finds her innocent of all charges. And further, the court orders that the subject will *never be brought up again* by any of the parties. So ordered."

"No worries. Make your jokes. I'm off to the coppers as soon as we're back in San Glendora."

"Fine. Do whatever you want."

"Contempt of court," said Neil quietly. "And you have that in spades, Samma my pet . . . the contempt of the court."

"I'll abide—for now."

"I'm sorry, girl," said Dwayne. I thought he was speaking to me and was about to berate him for calling me that—and for calling me Jeannie all those times—when I realized he was talking to Samma, of all people!

"What about?" she asked, suspiciously.

"I know you really believe what you're saying. But I had to vote my conscience."

Samma stared at Dwayne. I thought she was going to chow down on his head for breakfast . . . but then she actually *smiled* at the hunkster. "I'm not blaming you, exactly. I know you have to say what's in your heart."

"There's something else in my heart . . . but I've been afraid to say it. Until now."

She held her breath, waiting. Dwayne continued. "I know you're—taken; but if you weren't . . . you would be. I mean I would if you weren't—oh, you know what I mean!"

"I'm not," she whispered. "Not anymore. So I guess I am."

"You are."

"Then are we...?"

He nodded. "I think we are. I'd like to be . . . would you?"

"I'd like that!"

I freaked. I backed away from the sudden sprouting of emotion between them like I would from a heaping spoonful of saccharine. Assuming I had followed their ridiculous babbling, I had just witnessed a main-dude, main-babe proposal—and it was sickening!

I felt horribly offended . . . even though I would have given my wisdom teeth, if I still had them, to fob the Dwaynster off on someone, anyone, and Samma was as good a choice as any. Still, I felt like a dumped bride!

I almost said something about it; then common sense got the better of me, and I went and sat down next to my own main-dude—I mean, just a friend, really.

"Disgusting, isn't it?" I observed, quietly.

"Predictable. It won't last, though."

"Why not?"

"She'll start nagging him about siding with you, he'll fight back—she's not used to that—and they won't be speaking to each other in about an hour."

I sighed. "It was useful while it lasted."

I could have cut the tension with a knife, if I still had one. Neil's prediction came true, but it only took forty minutes. Then Samma said, "Dear heart, don't you think you might have been swayed just a mite by your gentlemanliness when you sided with Jeanette against me?" In two minutes, they were sitting back-to-back, fuming.

I sent Dwayne off for the wettest wood he could find; when he returned, I tried to talk him and Samma into doing the SOS thing again, using smoke signals this time . . . hoping the joint activity would bring them closer together again. I had started to get used to the idea of Dwayne and Samma being an item: they deserved each other. And they'd both leave me alone, then.

But the girl from Oz was having none of it, so Dwayne and I took up the slack.

I liked the way the smoke rose in the still, sullen air. Three small puffs, like cotton balls, followed by three longer puffs and three more cotton balls. The smoke rose slowly; the air was hot and humid. It plateaued a few hundred feet above our heads and spread out. I hoped the height we got before smearing was enough; it didn't seem very high.

"Maybe we should make a what-do-you-call-it," suggested Dwayne. "For Neil."

"What?" I was totally lost.

"You know, a thing-a-ma-jig."

"What—what—*what?*"

"You know, you ride in it!"

"Wheelchair? Dogsled? Amphibious landing craft?"

He shook the trashbag in frustration, totally messing up our S. "You carry wounded people in it!"

"Oh, a *litter!* Is that what you mean?"

"Yeah, that thing! We should make one, so we can carry Neil down the mountain and across the plain."

The cargo itself spoke up. "Dwayne, I don't think you realize what you're saying. The rivers are still swollen; I doubt we could even get past Sutter Stream, which is probably like the Mississippi River now. And there's mud so deep, if you fall down you can drown in it. And it's a long, long way back to San Glendora; took us three days to get here, and that was on a dry trail carrying nothing but our packs."

"Have you thought about one other point, Mr. Schwartzenegger?" I asked.

"What?"

I looked left and right conspiratorially. "If you've got one end—and Neil's on the litter—who carries the other end?"

Hey, I'm a strong girl, and Samma is no fashion-model wimp. But neither one of us was equipped by nature to haul an open-faced Neil Armstrong sandwich across twenty-five miles of swamp.

Dwayne opened his mouth to answer a couple of times, then shut it again, puzzled. It must be so nice to be a Viking— just smash your way though every problem with no responsibility to actually think a plan through and make it work.

I'll tell you the kind of macho *I* like: I like a guy you can rely on. I like a guy who tells the truth. I like a guy who *tells me what he's thinking!* I like a guy who keeps his commitments and takes responsibility.

I'd like a guy who would take care of us-as-a-team, not take care of me as a helpless child . . . and definitely not just take care of himself.

I wanted a smart guy, a guy who has the guts to talk when he should and shut up when he must. . . .

My face turned beet red—I could just feel it.

I wanted Neil Armstrong—present company, not the astronaut.

I had the weirdest sort of feeling, like I'd swallowed a balloon and it inflated a little bit more with every breath. It was totally bizarro to suddenly think of Neil-the-friend as Neil-the-boyfriend. But I felt such a surge of righteous *YES!* through my whole body when I asked me if I really wanted him that way that I knew it wasn't just a dweeby crush.

I knew something else, too: I knew he was in love with me in return. He may not have known it yet; I figured I'd have to beat it into his thick skull. But he was smart and trainable . . . he'd learn.

When I started itching to get my hands on him and mold him into even a better man than he already was, I knew it was official. As soon as you start molding and shaping, you've found the guy.

Of course, a slight problem remained: now that I had him, how was I to carry him home? I didn't bring a bag.

Neil was looking thoughtful, trying to figure out a way to boost the signaling capacity of the fire; Dwayne was staring at Samma with a mixture of longing and loathing; Samma was trying to look totally indifferent. Only I was staring eastward, toward where Neil said he'd heard a helicopter a few days ago . . . where the searchers were searching and the rescuers rescuing.

And I saw a black dot. *Bird? Frog?* I was afraid to think of the other possibility in case I jinxed it. But Miss Taylor jumped to conclusions: *it's a plane!*

I stared so hard at the dot, watching it grow, willing it to be a Beechcraft, that my dry and gritty contact lenses, already extended long past their extended-wear lifespan, rotated out of focus. I couldn't see a damn thing.

I looked away, frantically blinking my eyes, trying to get them to tear up. When I finally got the right eye to rotate back into position (I have an astigmatism), I covered my left eye and looked back at my spot.

At first, I couldn't find it—I'd lost it! Then I spotted it.

"A plane," I whispered, hoarse and unable to catch my breath.

"Maybe a plain if we could bend it concave," mused Neil.

"No, a plane—a plane!—*A PLANE, A PLANE!*"

My hysterical shrieking finally caught everyone's attention, and they fell over themselves trying to see.

It was, it was, by God, a fixed-wing aircraft—coming straight toward us! Us! Here, right toward the stranded kids on the mountaintop!

I heard the engine whine, faintly at first. . . .

Fourteen

Neil saw the plane and began screaming like a banshee, waving his arms. He stood, pulling himself up on his crutches, just as Dwayne and Samma crushed close around us.

I realized we were freaking, and I tried to jump in front of Neil to shield him from the out-of-control behemoth and the girl from Oz, neither of whom was paying any attention to poor, wounded Neil. But I may as well have bravely thrown myself in between the peanut and the freight train—not to compare Neil to a peanut, except when compared to Dwayne Cors.

Dwayne pounded into my back like a football player—not surprising—and I caromed off him right into my newly discovered beloved. Neil crashed to the ground beneath us . . . beneath *me*.

His face turned white as paper. His eyes flew open, and his mouth moved wordlessly. "Neil!" I shrieked. "Look out Dwayne, you rampaging bull!"

With the strength of desperation, I pushed my hand out and shoved Dwayne back.

Alas, my aim was a little too good, and by sheer mischance I happened to punch him, as Danny DeVito says in *Throw Momma From the Train,* "right in the gentles."

Dwayne staggered away, utterly convinced I'd done it on purpose in retaliation. It was all right; Samma did enough leaping about and hollering for the four of us, while I cradled Neil's head in my arms.

The pain must have been overwhelming; after a few seconds scrunching up his face and gritting his teeth, my love passed out.

I watched the plane as I held him. It was an old, high-wing Cessna, but it wasn't painted like an official aircraft: not sheriff, fire department, SAR, or military. It looked like a private plane. When it circled into the sunlight, I saw KNBC Channel 4 painted on the side, the local NBC affiliate—a news plane!

Samma dashed to the fire, grabbed a burning brand in each hand, and held them aloft like she was signaling a touchdown. Then she waved them in parallel back and forth, careful not to cross them. I don't know if it meant anything to her, but the pilot continued to circle.

The wind was so strong, it almost blew out Samma's torches. Obviously the plane couldn't land; there was no runway or anything like a runway. And I started to worry that it might be too steep and windy on the mountaintop to land a helicopter.

The only possibility that made any sense was for us to get down the mountain and wait for the helo on the flat ground. "Samma!" I shouted. "Tell him we're going to go down the north face of the peak and wait for the helicopter. Tell him!"

She did a lot of waving, and I had no idea whether the pilot understood a word of it. But she kept pointing north, and we could always build another signal fire.

After circling five or six more times, probably fixing our position on his navigational charts, the pilot leveled off back the way he came, wiggling his wings.

As he flew away, Dwayne, who had finally regained his breath and voice, started shouting, "Wait! Come back! We're here, we need help, damn you!"

"Dwayne," I said quietly, "he can't hear you, you know. He'll be back, don't worry—or a helicopter, probably."

He stared at me, unconsciously covering his crotch. "Assassin!" he hissed.

"What did she do?" demanded Samma. "Did she attack you?"

"Yeah, Samma," I said. "I was trying to keep him from signaling the plane, so I could kill you all at my leisure."

"You keep your hands off him! Haven't you done enough damage, Taylor?"

I turned my back on the woman who once was my

best, closest girlfriend. Neil was still unconscious. "We've got worse problems," I said quietly. "We've got a few hours to get down the hill . . . and not long after that to get Neil to a hospital. I think his broken bone nicked his femoral artery . . . I think he's bleeding into his leg."

Instantly, Samma became like totally professional. She squatted, feeling his pulse and trying to guess his blood pressure with no instruments. Neil's skin was cold and clammy, still very white, and he didn't respond to being pinched. "You're right," she agreed soberly, "he needs to be in a hospital—like yesterday."

"Maybe I should make that litter after all," said Dwayne.

"No time, Dwayne-dude. We've got to get down the mountain and find some flat, sheltered spot where a helo can land."

Dwayne took Neil under the arms, and I took his good leg; Samma took the injured leg, since she had more first-aid training than either Dwayne or me.

We walked Neil northward, Samma trying to remember exactly where the trail began. We reached the slope, but it was too steep to carry Neil down. Samma led us along the perimeter until she found a landmark she vaguely recognized. There, the ground wasn't quite as steep: it was still a bitch, but we might be able to get Neil down the hill if we were careful.

I couldn't help being amazed by the view. The sky had cleared; there wasn't a cloud. Bright, golden sunlight reflected so brightly from the glassy, wet grasslands below that I had to squint my eyes against it. I wished I still had my blue-block sunglasses, but they'd been lost in the very first tidal punch of flood-waters. The sun gilded the distant, perpetually snow-capped peaks of the El Camino mountain range, where we should have been . . . and whence we'd have been picked up days and days ago, if we'd planned our hike and hiked our plan.

Tears slowly rolled down my cheeks as we picked a path through the scrubbrush and ivy that over-grew the faintly discernible trail. I convinced myself they were just my eyes' belated attempt to moisten the contacts; but I was feeling powerful emotions about finally leaving this serene, peaceful, deadly, brutal, challenging, exalting place.

I kind of didn't want to leave. I was kind of afraid to return to the ordinary world of school and Jaq, Mom and pictures of Dad . . . and Neil next door. I was sort of, kind of afraid of how everything was going to change, now that I realized he was no longer just my best buddy across the picket fence.

The trail followed a ridge that switched back and forth as it slithered down the Hag's Tooth, but it was better than scaling the cliff. We saw no place safe for a helicopter to land. Every jarring step caused Neil to wince; I hoped that meant he was coming out of his stupor . . . and after about half-an-hour, he moaned, then tried to talk—babble, really. But after a few minutes, he was semicoherent.

"They found us," I said immediately; I figured, may as well give him the good news right away, give him something to fight for. He didn't understand at first; then he seemed to get it.

"Coming?" he asked.

"Yes, my love; they're coming."

"Coming?"

"Yes, they're coming." I was prepared to tell him as many times as it would take until it sunk in.

Dwayne, who was carrying most of Neil's weight, had to stop frequently and put him down to rest. About an hour after we started down the trail, Neil struggled up to a sitting position after Dwayne put him down. "I think I can walk," he said. He sounded weak, but again the old Neil.

We hadn't brought the crutches, of course. Dwayne was angry—he'd spent some time making them, and here we'd just left them upstairs!

"When's that helicopter coming back?" asked Dwayne, squinting eastward.

"Maybe another hour or so," I guessed. "At this point, it doesn't matter . . . unless we find somewhere we can be picked up, it can come right now and it wouldn't do us any good."

"It doesn't have to land, you know," whispered Neil.

"What? What do you mean?"

"I mean, Jet Stream, it can hover and winch us up, one by one."

"Or at least Neil," added Samma, feeling his leg. I had no idea what she was feeling for . . . swelling?

Temperature? "The rest of us can wait a few more hours while they get Neil to a hospital, now that we know they're coming back for us." She looked at me coldly. "For *most* of us."

I didn't respond. Samma was below my radar now and forever more.

The slope of the mountain took the base quite a bit farther ahead of us. But not too far below was a meadow, still on the shoulder . . . and still at a steep-ish slope, but possibly level enough for the helo. It was a possible abort site, in case we didn't have time to continue all the way to the bottom.

We carried Neil a bit more, but his protestations got louder and angrier; finally, Samma reluctantly gave her permission for Neil to walk, supported on either side by me and Dwayne.

He kept his broken leg up and hopped—hissing in pain with each step. But it was a lot faster and less tiring than carrying him.

"Neil, honey," I said, "what's the first thing you're going to do when you get back?"

"You mean before or after they amputate my leg?"

"Don't be stupid! It's just a broken leg. You don't have a snakebite or anything."

He grinned; but it was more of a grimace. "I don't know, Jet; it feels bad. Really bad. I've been thinking about it . . . I don't want to lose my leg; but if it's— Jesus." I waited until the pain subsided; then he continued. "But if it's a choice between my leg and my life, it's not even a question."

"You'll be all right, Neil; you won't lose the leg."

"Promise?"

I pressed my lips together. I know the sympathetic thing to do would have been to promise him; but Neil and I had a funny relationship. We couldn't lie to each other—and I couldn't make that kind of promise! I smiled and shrugged.

"Dearest," he gasped; I leaned close to hear, secretly thrilled that he called me that. He had never called me a term of endearment before. "I think you'd better leave me here and let me rest a bit."

"Leap! We're not going to leave you behind!"

"Don't be ridiculous. You know how selfish I am . . . you think I'd suggest some braindead act of altruism? I just meant leave me behind while you scout the rest of the trail, make sure you can find it."

"Oh." A few more steps, and we found a large rock. We leaned Neil up against it and propped his leg upon a rock, so it would drain; then Dwayne and I continued down the trail, practically running . . . just slow enough not to do the Jack and Jill number. Jeez, that would be all we needed . . . two broken heads to go along with Neil's broken leg!

Because of the switchbacks, the trail led us on for another mile and a half . . . and then it just ended! I skidded to a halt, windmilling my arms and dancing over a sixty-foot drop; I was one hundred percent convinced that Dwayne was going to slam into me, caroming me into a graceful swan dive into the rushing river water below. Thank God he was far enough behind that he stopped and pulled me back.

A river? Another river—or the same stupid one that blocked us on the other side?

I was getting so sick and tired of rivers, I can't even tell you. If I never saw another river or flooded marshland again, it would be years too soon.

"Jesus," whispered Dwayne, "the trail's gone!"

"Good eyes, kiddo. Washed away, I figure. See? It starts up again about thirty yards farther down."

"But Neil and—and Samma came up this way. How could it...?"

"Well, obviously the water kept eating away at it until it undercut the bank. Or a log hit it. Or Mideast terrorists bombed it . . . how the hell would I know? Christ!"

"Uh . . . now what, Jeannie?"

I glared coldly. All right, if that was his game: "Now, *Dwaynie,* I guess we go back upstairs and take Plan B, the meadow."

We carefully picked our way up the trail; the ground was wet, muddy, and very slippery, and I didn't want to slip'n'slide right over the cliff.

We returned the way we came; but of course, it took much longer going up than down. Hiking magazines are always saying it's harder going down a trail than up; but I think they've been smoking something funny. That's total nonsense! It's *much* harder going up; you've got that ol' devil gravity to fight against going up. I was totally exhausted after we had climbed only halfway; it was only by sucking down the rest of the waterbottle full of muddy liquid and screaming in frustration that I was able to continue on without stopping.

Dwayne had no trouble.

Back at the ranch, I broke the news to Neil and Samma . . . and I pointed out Jeanette's Meadow as a possible alternate LZ, or landing zone.

Neil was skeptical. "I . . . don't think a helo can set down there, Jet; it's too steep, and it's probably wet and slick. But maybe it can hover."

"Well," I said, cupping my hands over my eyes, "we'd better do something quick: here comes the Seventh Cavalry."

I saw a tiny dot in the distance. Well, two dots, actually; my contact lenses always gave me two images for very tiny, very faint objects . . . like stars. There was only one helicopter.

"One?" demanded Dwayne, outraged. "That's all we rate? *One* chopper?"

"That's probably all they had at the nearest base of OpCenter," said Neil; his voice was still very weak, and he sagged ominously against the rock. "I'm sure other helos will be coming in another half hour or so."

"You're going in that one," I declared. Samma said much the same thing at the same moment, and Dwayne didn't object.

"All right," I decided. "It's the meadow. Last one there's a major butthead."

Dwayne and I each got one of Neil's arms over our

shoulders, and we started out, trying to keep separate eyes on the trail, Neil, and the bird. I wished that Dwayne's father, who had equipped his son (unknowingly) with the MREs that had kept us alive for a couple of days, had also equipped him with colored smoke grenades . . . but like they say, "If wishes were horses, beggars would eat."

By the time we got close to the meadow, I realized that Neil was right: besides being steep, the stupid ground was covered with about a foot and a half of deep mud! "This sucks," I said, pulling my foot loose for another step; but nobody got it, or they didn't think it was funny.

At least we could get far enough away from the mountainside that the helo wouldn't be bashed against a rock and explode. And the wind was in the west, so we were somewhat leeward.

I waited, heart pounding in time with the beat of the rotors, while the beautiful, beautiful silver helicopter hovered closer and closer, finally spotting us and rushing over. The words SAN NICHOLAS COUNTY FIRE DEPARTMENT RESCUE emblazoned the side of his canopy.

The driver started circling, trying to decide whether he dared set the bird down. He descended low enough that he could see how we were slogging through mud, and that evidently decided him.

"Attention hikers," he roared through a PA system. "Jeanette Taylor, please wave your arms."

I did as instructed, and he worked through the

rest of our names, calling Bill Hicks second to last. The pilot continued to circle, sizing up the situation.

"One person come aboard to help winch up the injured party," boomed the pilot's PA system.

Dwayne looked at me; I looked at Samma, who looked at Neil. "You skit, Taylor," she said, sounding detached. "I'll stick 'round with *him* until they come back."

"Yeah," agreed my hunklike ex-worshipper, "maybe we need some time alone together."

The pilot had more helpful advice: "Be aware of the cliff edge," he thundered. Like I wouldn't have noticed.

The meadow sloped downward, leading to the lip of a very steep slope . . . not quite a sheer cliff, like we climbed, but steep enough to dump an unlucky tobogganer into whichever river circled the north face of the Hag's Tooth now.

I moved away from the other three, and Neil gave me a thumb's up. "Thanks," I said.

"No, you dweeb—I mean give thumb's up to the pilot!"

"Oh!" I turned to the pilot and gave the signal huge enough that he could see it from thirty feet up.

The wind from the rotors was blowing like a hurricane as he reached over and threw a horse collar out the open side door. A "horse collar" is actually for rescuing people, but it looks like the thing they used to put on horses to draw carts back in olden times.

I guess there must have been more of a breeze

than I thought, for the collar swung wildly. The helo driver seemed to have a hard time holding his hover, which worried me. My stomach tightened up a bit as the horse collar swung past my head. I dove for it but missed, ending up on my knees in the mud. Oh well, at least it gave Neil a chuckle.

I snagged it on the second pass. I'd seen how you were supposed to worked these things in movies: you duck inside and face the rope, so the padded part of the collar loops around behind your back; then you hold the rope . . . that way, you can't fall out.

I started to do it, but the helicopter surged in a sudden gust. I held tight to the collar, and it actually started to lift me into the air! I was just about to drop it before I got too high, when the bird settled a bit. My feet sank into the mud . . . quickly, before another gale whipped around the mountain, I threw the collar over my head and got in position, giving another thumb's up.

But as I gripped the steel cable, I convulsed and screamed . . . I caught the biggest static-electrical shock I'd ever felt in my life! I thought I was going to fry. I'm surprised my hair didn't stand on end.

Suddenly, I was off the ground, fighting back yet another scream, this one just for being a girl; but I didn't succumb—I gritted my teeth the whole way up and kept my eyes open. If I ever wanted to try to become a test pilot and maybe an astronaut—and with Neil Armstrong around, who could avoid thinking about it?—I had to learn to take dramatic rescues in stride.

In moments, I was thirty feet off the ground, my legs dangling, feeling the wind kick me all over the place and every which way but upside-down. The cable looped up to a small crane arm sticking out the side of the craft; when the collar bumped up against it, I grabbed the crane and piked my legs up and into the helo. . . .

And I was rescued, by God.

Wow. The pilot leaned back and shouted to me. I could barely hear him over the high-pitched whine of the engines and the steady chopping of the rotors. "Unhook the collar," he bellowed, "and pull that Stokes over here!"

I didn't know what a Stokes was until I remembered that ancient TV show *Emergency!,* from way before I was born; a Stokes is some kind of wire-mesh litter for transporting injured parties. I stared around the cramped cabin and realized I was sitting on it.

Trying not to tumble out the open door, I planted a foot on the gutter of each bulkhead and pulled the litter out from beneath me, handing it up to the pilot. I handed him the cable eye, and he let go the controls long enough to assure himself it was hooked in properly; I guess he didn't trust a civilian.

Then he grabbed the collective and the thingie-what-you-call-it, narrowly saving us from slipping sideways into the dirt.

He would answer to "Hi!" or to any loud cry
Such as "Fry me!" or "Fritter my wig!"
To "What-you-may-call-um!" or "What-was-his-name!"
But especially "Thing-um-a-jig!"

Lewis Carroll ringing in my head, I went a-snark hunting with the Stokes, trying to steady the line as it slowly lowered toward the ground. "Detach the litter and strap Mr. Armstrong inside," said the pilot over the PA, "then hook it back up, and I'll bring him aboard."

By the time it neared the ground, it was swinging like a pendulum. Dwayne fended it away from his face; then the pilot dropped it the last couple of feet into the mud.

Samma and Dwayne didn't bother unhooking the Stokes; they just scooped Neil up and dumped him inside. They didn't even strap him in!

I shouted and bellowed, but they couldn't hear me over the rotors and the wind, of course; I didn't have a public address system. The helo driver didn't realize the dangerous situation, and he began winching Neil up.

I was furious at the idiot San Nicholas Fire Department for not equipping their rescue helos with two guys, so one could jump out and strap Neil up right—why did they depend on the victims to do the dangerous work, for heaven's sake? I smelled lawsuit. . . .

Neil was awake enough to realize what was going

on. He grabbed hold of the sides of the metal basket just as the vicious wind picked him up and flung him into a crazy orbit on the end of his rope tether.

I leaned dangerously out the door, unstrapped, and tried to steady the cable; still, the wind caught the metal mesh like a kite and started it swinging wildly, spinning like a Yo-Yo when it runs out of yo. Overanxious, Samma Glynnis rushed toward the litter, trying to grab and steady it.

Big mistake.

Fifteen

Jack and Jill went up the hill
To fetch a pail of water;
Jack fell down and broke his crown,
And Jill came tumbling after!

O r in this case, Samma fell stiff and slid off a cliff. Jesus, what was I saying? Dork or no dork, she could be dead!

The litter jerked around, pounding Samma in the face. Samma screamed and grabbed her mouth, eyes wide . . . then she was clawing for a foothold, like a Rollerblader in an ice rink.

She went down hard on her butt and started sliding toward the edge. By the time she realized her danger, she was already moving too fast to stop by grabbing hold of the grass: She just ripped it out in clumps and continued down the hill.

"S-A-M-M-A!" bellowed Dwayne, slip-sliding down

the slope after her as fast as he could go, just barely keeping control of his own motion.

Silently, with a look of utter shock and astonishment, Samma slid over the edge of the cliff and vanished, bloody mouth and all.

I couldn't breathe; I felt an enormous hand clamped around my middle, squeezing the diaphragm so it wouldn't suck air into my lungs. Samma was gone! Just like that! It could happen to anyone; it could happen to Neil.

He dangled precariously by a mere metal thread.

For a moment, I considered trying to slide down the cable like Bruce Willis and strap Neil in; but that was a stupid idea. I didn't even know if the crane could take that much weight! The only thing I could do was watch breathlessly as the pilot slowly raised the Stokes, as Neil clung for grim life, as the cage swung back and forth, spun wildly, did everything but turn upside-down.

Dwayne hit the cliff and dug in his heels, grinding, to a messy, precarious halt on the edge of the abyss. Waving his arms to hold his balance, he stood and peeked over the side.

I couldn't see his expression; he was too far away. He turned toward the helo and shouted something, but it was lost in the noise.

Then the dumb, heroic idiot turned and *jumped off the cliff!*

I screamed—briefly—but there didn't seem any

sense in it, so I shut up. I already had someone to worry about.

Neil was most of the way up, so I concentrated on leaning down and catching hold of the hook and eyelet, trying to steady the litter and turn it the right way. But just toward the top, the mesh got away from me and a corner hooked on the edge of the landing skid.

The Stokes tilted halfway over, and my heart leapt into my throat—if Neil spilled out at this height, he would probably break the other leg . . . or his neck!

He felt what was happening and pressed away from the sinking side. Just as he started to slide out, I suddenly turned into the Incredible She-Hulk, reached down, and grabbed him by the arm.

I have never, never, never in my life been so grateful for learning how to do pull-ups. Otherwise . . . I would have lost my love ten minutes after finding him!

Take note: it's a cold and sexist world. Maybe Coach Leticia with the mustache will let you get by with a "bent-arm hang," but nature doesn't give a . . . a hang, I guess. Practice those pull-ups!

I braced one foot on the crane and the other on the lip of the door and bodily hauled Neil up and out of the litter, which was still caught on the skid. His eyes went wide, and he desperately tried to keep his mangled leg from banging against anything. He still wasn't all there, poor thing; I got him into the helo, then stepped carefully over him to lean over the pilot's shoulder, almost sending us into a nosedive in the process.

"Samma went over the cliff!" I hollered, pointing. I had to repeat it a couple of times, but he finally got the message and charged over to the spot where I'd last seen her and Dwayne.

We circled; at first I couldn't see a thing, then the helo driver spotted the two of them.

They were together; we dropped as close as we could. Samma was limp, her ridiculously punk-red hair turned almost brown by being waterlogged. She looked very white . . . almost blue.

I didn't think she was breathing.

Dwayne had his arm around her, grimly holding her steady against the horrific current, his other arm clutching a tree root as if his life, and hers, depended upon it.

It was a static tableau; Samma was out of it, and Dwayne couldn't let go of either hand to get her head above the water or get her breathing again. She was going to drown while we all watched!

The pilot shouted something unintelligible at me, but I was already unhooking the Stokes and chucking it overboard, attaching the horse collar again instead.

"Lower it!" I yelled. *"LOW—ER IT!"*

The driver activated the winch, and the collar started to sink; but the wind off the river kicked up and threw us violently side to side, so much so that the pilot freaked and gave the rotors some gas, raising us up thirty feet. Maybe he was afraid the blades would chop the kids into salami.

The collar dangled below us—I've always wanted to say this—twisting slowly, slowly in the wind. Actually, it spun out of control, flipping up to slap the canopy. For an instant, I thought it might foul the rotors . . . wouldn't that be great! Then we could all crash and burn, killed by our rescuer! The pilot quickly winched it back up against the crane.

Of course, said Miss Taylor, *it wouldn't spin anywhere near as much with some weight on it . . . say a hundred and twenty pounds?*

"I was just getting there," I retorted nervously. Liar! I'd been desperately hoping the collar would lower without incident.

It was a silly hope: what would Dwayne do with it if it had? He surely couldn't let go to make a grab at it.

I knew what we had to do—and I knew who had to do it.

"I'm getting into the collar—lower it again!" Either he didn't hear me or he didn't want to; in any case, I yanked the yellow, nylon ring over my head, hooked my arms over the top, and stood at the edge of the door.

I swallowed a couple of times. I prayed silently. And I fought the terrible urge to go to the bathroom— my father had told me about that embarrassing little problem when you faced imminent death; but I never believed him until then.

> *If you can keep your head when all about you*
> *Are losing theirs and blaming it on you. . . .*

I never much liked Kipling; but *If* was one of my favorite poems, except for the last line. I ignored the possibility of wetting myself; I was about to get a hell of a lot wetter!

I stepped off the lip and found myself dangling over the churningest river I'd ever seen up close and personal.

Free from the bird, I swung like the pendulum on a grandmother clock, back and forth, up and down, until I was about four-tenths seasick. It never occurred to me to bring Dramamine on a mountain hike.

I kept dipping lower and lower as the frightened pilot lowered me into the deadly water; whenever a rage of wind grabbed the helo, it surged in some random direction: it might drop me toward the river in freefall; it yanked me up toward the mountaintop; it tried to dash me against the rocks on the side . . . Grease-Smears "R" Us. I tried closing my eyes, but that was a hundred times worse! I was as gutsy as the Cowardly Lion.

Then with one of the gusts, I dropped straight into the water. What a shock—it was cold as a San Francisco morning in February. Now I knew how those prisoners trying to escape Alcatraz by swimming the bay felt.

The current caught me and ripped me down-stream; since the cable held me tight, I kicked up a huge spray three times as high as my head above the water. It arced over me like a fountain, splashing back into the river right about where Dwayne held the dying Samma.

He turned to look at where the sudden waterfall was coming from and spotted me. The pilot drifted slowly forward—I had no idea you could handle a helicopter so delicately in a hurricane—and drifted me right up next to the guys.

I rolled with the current and let myself drift right up on top of Samma, who was just starting to hack and cough; she still didn't look sure where she was or why she was all wet, but at least she wasn't quite so blue.

I slammed into the girl a bit harder than I intended; the shock almost jarred her from Dwayne's grasp, but he hung on.

I wrapped my arms and legs around Samma Glynnis. *"Tell the pilot we're okay!"* I screamed into Dwayne's ear.

Naturally, he raised his head and bellowed the message into the churning rotor blades. Thanks, Dwayne!

"No, you dweeb—flash him the okay sign!"

Dwayne started to comply then realized he would have to let go of either Samma or the tree root. *"It's all right,"* I added, *"I've got her! But I can't unhook my arms or legs!"*

Staring with suspicion, as if he thought it might be a trick, Dwayne gingerly let go of Samma . . . but he kept his hand right nearby, ready to snatch at her hair if I let her go. After a few seconds, he finally believed that it was safe and dared to flash the pilot the okay signal, making a circle with a thumb and forefinger.

"Make a circle with your arm and touch the top of your head," I shouted.

Dwayne did as I told him, and the helo gunned its engines. It lifted slowly into the air, the driver nervous because he was holding two rescues on the end of his cable; I don't think the system was designed for it.

The winch ground so loudly that I could hear it over the pulsing, pounding noise of the helo itself; we rose with aching slowness, and I was sincerely worried that we'd exceeded the capacity of the equipment. But if we had, I don't think the pilot would be fool enough to winch us up anyway. I had to assume he knew what he was doing.

Samma weighed a metric ton. I kept my arms and legs locked, but they felt like they were being pulled out of their sockets! I scissored my legs so hard, I was afraid Samma wouldn't be able to breathe . . . again; but I was more afraid of dropping her into the river to be swept away into the vastly deep, like Bill Hicks.

As soon as we were clear of the water, the pilot slid the helicopter sideways until we dangled over swampland rather than a raging river. I saw Dwayne, unencumbered by damsels in distress, pull himself out of the river and sit up in the mud like a lady wrestler at the Ticonderoga Nightclub. He'd be all right for the next few hours until we could come back and fetch him.

I don't know how I managed to hang onto Samma; she was deadweight, and I was dead-dog exhausted.

The whining of the machinery got so loud as we approached the minicrane that I wanted to cover my ears; but of course, I needed two hands, two legs, and a prehensile tail to hold onto my ex–best-girlfriend.

Finally, we jerked to a stop; I opened my eyes and saw the doorway right next to me. I started the cable swinging a few times, trying to work up the courage. Finally, when I swung slightly into the cab of the helocopter, I unhooked my feet, dropping Samma none too gently onto the deckplates. As soon as I was sure she was inside, I let go my arms as well, then struggled inside after her.

"Strap 'em down!" ordered the pilot. I found a couple of sets of ordinary looking seat belts . . . didn't they even use special, helicopter equipment for that? I got Neil strapped in; he wasn't moving around much. But Samma was trouble. She was about two-thirds awake, and her natural Aussie stubborn

streak chose that moment to take over; she refused the seat belt, slurring something about the "car" flipping over and burning.

Well, that's stupid even in a car, but it's downright braindead in an open-doored helicopter! I leaned heavily against her and strapped her down.

The only problem was that there wasn't really a third seat for me; Neil and Samma took up too much room.

"Stay where you are!" boomed the pilot over the PA system, talking to Dwayne, of course. "Do not move! Do not stray from this spot! A rescue unit will be here soon to take you home! Don't move, stay where you are!"

An exhausted Dwayne Cors looked up and feebly made a big circle with his arm, touching the top of his head. The pilot gunned it and sped away eastward.

> *If you can force your heart and nerve and sinew*
> *To serve your turn long after they are gone,*
> *And so hold on when there is nothing in you*
> *Except the Will which says to them: "Hold on!"*

I didn't expect the helicopter to shake and rattle so, an airborne earthquake; having grown up here in Northern Cal, I felt right at home. I couldn't really find a good seat, so I shoehorned myself in between Neil and Samma, facing backward and getting progressively more airsick, trying not to bump Neil's leg even when we unexpectedly hit isotherms and wind gusts and the beast lurched violently either to one side or the other, or up or down.

It was loud, too. Talking was a bear . . . or it would have been, if Samma and I had been talking to each other. After a while, the constant noise started to sound like an echo chamber, or a deep cavern far underground—the grinding, scraping sound of a merry-go-round falling apart. An end-of-the-world noise. Everything winding down, but loudly. Everyone talking at the end of a play, talking over the final lines. I felt tiny and insignificant, like all of a sudden I was my little brother Jaq and the grown-ups were driving me around in the car, not telling me where we were going or why.

It was a dreadful feeling, and I knew just what it was: I was leaving one universe forever behind, heading for a new one, a new-old universe I once lived in that would never be the same again. The terrible, shaking echo was the noise on the inside of a wormhole to the universe next door.

I stared backward at the wilderness wasteland unrolling, receding behind us like the plains of Central Africa when you're flying back to civilization. So long to the Serengeti, and hello "home."

What a weird thought. I hadn't thought about San Glendora in a couple of thousand years, not since I looked up to see Bill Hicks spying on me from beneath a particularly ugly rock. Civilization itself meant nothing since sometime before I turned down the forest mushrooms and we found Dwayne merrily relieving himself in a clearing.

The girl who had hunted rabbit and kilt her a b'ar was not the same girl who had to get up mornings to stumble downstairs, push a bowl of cereal down her throat, and toddle off to Andrew Johnson High School to study all about Neanderthal Man.

If you can fill the unforgiving minute
With sixty seconds' worth of distance run,
Yours is the Earth and everything that's in it,
And—which is more—you'll be a Man, my son!

Yeah, today I am a man. Hell, it was just as silly to say today I was a woman. I didn't have any idea what I was going to do with my life; I was a mediocre-to-good student, but I didn't have the grades for Princeton or Yale or even good ol' Stanford, just up the road. I was headed to UC Berkeley if I was lucky, or more likely Santa Cruz. I could major in psychology and sit on a chair the rest of my working career, scribbling down the disturbing thoughts of disturbed patients.

The helo lurched again, and we were thrown into another alternate timeline; in this one, I joined the Marines right out of high school and served for a few years. Congress changed the law so I got trained as an infantryman; then we went to war in Bosnia, and I got my intestines shot out by a Serbian soldier who didn't know any more than me about why he was there shooting at people.

All right, so it wouldn't be a bad way to die, as deaths go. Maybe it would be quick, even if not exactly painless.

But I didn't really want to die at all; not ever.

In the hundredth history, Samma suddenly spoke. I thought I was just dreaming it again; but it was real.

"Taylor, I . . . I just wanted to say. . . ."

"So say it." I wasn't in a charitable mood. Samma had interrupted a timeline where, due to an incredible mix-up, I had become Mrs. Mel Gibson; and I wanted to see whether anyone caught on.

"Thanks loads."

"Sure. Don't mention it." Mel was fading, fading fast. . . .

"No, I mean thanks awfully. That took some brass ones, jumping in like that. You didn't have to; a real Jillaroo."

"Nothing personal." Oh *God,* were we catty today!

Samma shut up, but it was too late; my husband had abandoned me for another timeline where I became a world-famous heart surgeon.

Then she spoke up again; this time, I was grateful for the interruption, since I can't stand the sight of blood, especially someone else's.

"Taylor—Jeanette—I guess I take it back. You're not a killer, else you'd not be leaping into the drink after me. Especially not me, not after I said I'd sic the coppers on you. You'd've let me drown—no worries! Dead men tell no tales, and that.

"So I've decided I won't talk to the police. I believe you about that right bastard Bill. And if they ask, I'll just say I wasn't there, so how could I know? Deal, right?"

"Right." I was too tired to have any sort of emotional reaction at all, except for my pervasive sense of unreality, that I wasn't really all there—either the universe or I was fuzzy around the edges.

Right. Well, that took care of one worry; but it didn't solve the problem. The problem hadn't changed. How the heck was I going to explain to Mother Dearest and Bill's parents—and yes, the cops—just how I happened to kill poor Bill Hicks?

I was wrong; I did have an emotional reaction. Extreme, silent terror.

I left the land of rebirth and headed back toward the land of my birth, leaving two messes behind: a dead Bill and a very alive Dwayne.

And a very, very dead Alfred, Lord Tennyson . . .

Most weary seemed the sea, weary the oar,
Weary the wandering fields of barren foam.
Then some one said, "We will return no more";
And all at once they sang, "Our island home
Is far beyond the wave; we will no longer roam."

The helo lurched again; we entered yet another timeline, one where we floated above a pad with flashing lights and about a hundred paramedics, searchers, news crews, and cops, cops, cops, cops, cops.

Sixteen

O r, if you prefer, Byron:

> *So we'll go no more a-roving*
> *So late into the night,*
> *Though the heart be still as loving,*
> *And the moon be still as bright.*

We slammed down on the pad, and "that's put an end tae her rovin'," as the old Irish song says. I stared out the windowless window, wondering what on earth I was going to tell them . . . not just the cops, and not just about Bill Hicks. What do you say to aliens from another planet? That's sort of what they were; their deep, important concerns were my faintly remembered trivia for the last couple of weeks, almost. And my day-to-day urgent considerations were water, food, shelter, safety, and the up-to-the-minute intrigues of my tribe—we spoke a different language.

Seen in that context, the death of Bill Hicks was just a failed attempt by a tribal warrior to seize control of the chiefdom from me . . . but I knew enough not to say *that* aloud— never!

The many-headed crushed around the helo without even a concern for getting those many heads chopped off by the whirling blades; nobody did, of course. But the police and firefighters couldn't keep them back. I mean, we were *big* news, like if they actually found Tarzan of the Apes hiding in the California outback.

Samma screamed and bent over at the waist, hiding her face in her hands. Being from a big city like Melbourne, you'd think she was used to huge mobs; they didn't give her the creepy feeling I got every time I went to the city, I mean San Francisco, or the one time I visited Los Angeles (I didn't like it except for Disneyland, but I was eleven then).

The reporters didn't see me at first. They were no respecters of Samma's privacy; they shoved mikes into her face and tried to pry her hands away . . . but she cursed at them with a long string of profanity that sure impressed the hell out of me but wouldn't make it onto the six o'clock news, I reckoned. Even the newsies drew the line at trying to interview Neil, who lay back moaning unresponsively (except for somebody from *Hard Copy*, who kept asking him whether he planned to sue the county for something or other).

With a curious motion, cameras and reporters began jerking back from us as if we'd suddenly turned into two-headed mutants. Then I realized the cops were yanking them away and "escorting" them back behind the yellow police tape—that's a polite euphemism for twisting arms behind backs and using martial-art "come-alongs" to propel the news hounds a few dozen feet back.

I felt like a criminal as I bolted out of the helo, covering my face with my arm to avoid being splashed across the San Glendora Tributary, except I would probably be printed just like that (and probably over the caption "Student Teen Denies All Charges"). A pair of paramedics, one female and one male, crushed in on either side of me with their arms around my waist and hauled me into a waiting ambulance for my first, and I hope only ride to the hospital with screaming sirens and flashing lights.

They'd put Samma into the same medical van, but Neil was somewhere else ... hopefully with painkillers into him by then. Samma and I sat on opposite sides of the van, trying not to see each other.

She looked at me once, her eyes asking 'can you forgive me? can we be friends again?'

I let my face, cold as stone, answer for me.

I knew her apology had been sincere. I knew she

finally believed me. But it didn't make any difference. I wasn't lying when I told Neil I demanded *total loyalty* from my friends; and Samma Glynnis had failed me when I most needed her support.

She was dead to me. She would always be dead.

We were in the tail ambulance. I looked out the back window to avoid looking at Samma and saw an enormous caravan of at least *forty cars! Cop cars, news vans, big, expensive* Lexuses and Mercedes—politicians?—and a couple of dozen other vehicles of God knows who. All of a sudden, Jeanette Taylor was the most famous person in the whole county of San Nicholas, barony of San Glendora, and they hadn't even heard about Bill yet.

Just wait, promised Miss Taylor; *prepare yourself—it's going to get a lot worse, believe me.*

My first inkling of The Question happened just as we rolled up the hospital driveway (everyone else except for the police went around to the visitors' entrance). In the few minutes from the pad, the efficient rescue paramedics had managed to feel my pulse, measure my blood pressure with a cuff and stethoscope, take my temperature with a digital thermometer, and unbutton my flannel shirt to listen to my heart beat, my belly, my back, my lungs, my shoulders, spine, and everything else that might make noises. Then, while the woman gagged me with one of those Popsicle-stick tongue depressors and spelunked down my throat with a torch helmet, she asked what had happened to the other two kids.

I told her about Dwayne; he was still back at the LZ and would be rolling in, in a couple of hours, as soon as somebody flew back and picked him up. Then I took a deep breath, dodged another probe from the tongue-stick, and told her about Bill Hicks.

I decided halfway through the story that my only chance for freedom—and self-respect—was to tell the absolute, total truth from Hour-Zero. "The other kid, Bill Hicks, won't be coming back. He went crazy and tried to kill me while we were climbing a cliff, and—and I kicked him and he fell. He's dead."

There was a silent beat while the two paramedics paused, absorbing the intelligence. Then they resumed, now with the icy, professional calm they beat into them at paramedical school.

"Is that what happened?" I heard the guy paramedic quietly ask Samma; true to her word, she said, "I didn't see dot; we hadn't latched up yet."

I stuck to the story—word for word—when the male paramedic asked me The Question while I sat in the hospital room waiting for the doctor. I said the same thing when Dr. Juliette Rhysling asked me what happened to Bill. Then the hospital psychologist wandered by—just "checking" on us after our ordeal—and I told him the same thing. All this long before the cops said anything to me . . . but I know they were listening just outside the room, because I saw them down the hall when I went inside.

If you've never been in a hospital—don't! Well, only if you're very sick. It's a sickening place . . . literally. In the few, brief hours I sat there, being poked and prodded by every metallic instrument of torture ever used by Tomás de Torquemada, all of them just removed from the freezer, I managed to catch strep. Oh yes, you can get sick *in* a hospital; it's a big building stuffed full of trillions of different germs . . . and maybe a doctor or two, here and there.

The door burst open. The nurse hanging with me tried to protest, but very little short of a tank trap or a bank-vault door can stop Mother Dearest when she gets a plan in her head . . . and at the moment, her plan was to roll right over the next person who tried to stop her seeing her kid.

The nurse-lady got as far as "I'm sorry, visiting hours—" when she was straight-armed out of the way, and then my mother was all over me like a warm, furry jacket . . . and you know, I didn't mind a bit. I didn't care that it was uncool. I wanted my mother.

When she swept me into her arms, not saying a thing, all of a sudden I didn't have a doubt in the world which timeline I wanted to be in for the rest of my life. I'd kept all these emotions at bay while in the wasteland; I couldn't afford to think about her (or even Jaq) because I'd have started crying and feeling miserable, and I had people to keep alive—including myself.

But I didn't have any responsibilities now—and all the feelings flooded out into Mom's arms. I know I cried, but I was really beyond tears. I just wanted her, like suddenly I was four years old again and some big kid had scared me before I pounded him.

She made meaningless, soothing noises and patted my head and stuff, and then would you believe it? I had to tell the Bill Hicks story all over again. Mother Dearest sat next to me quietly and didn't interrupt, and when I finished, she put her arms around my shoulders and spoke so quietly I could barely hear her.

"Honey, I believe you. I know you're a good kid, and you wouldn't ever do anything like what you did unless it was a life or death situation. And I would have done the same thing . . . and your dad is proud of you too, upstairs.

"But for right now—Jeanette, this is really, really important—I don't want you saying a word to the police. Not a word—nothing! I called Martin Booth, our attorney; he's on his way. Don't even talk to the police until he gets here, then do whatever he says. Do you understand me, hon?"

"I understand, Mom."

"Not a word! Not until the lawyer is here."

"I got it. I won't talk until Booth gets here, and I'll say whatever he tells me to say."

I really felt relieved. It was getting pretty tired of telling everyone in the world about what happened, and the more I told it, the stranger it sounded, even to me! Although I knew in my head what I said was the truth, the words started sounding more hollow with every retelling.

It was good to have a solid reason to bag it for a while, especially before going and talking to the police, a prospect that was steadily panicking me the more I thought about it. I don't know why; I didn't do anything wrong.

Well, I do know why: what if they didn't believe me? Even Samma had thought I was a psycho-killer from hell, and the cops didn't even know me.

I kept asking random doctors and nurses about Dwayne, and finally one of them told me he was back and in the hospital. I asked about Samma; she was all right, though they wanted to keep her overnight because of the near-drowning.

And she was currently with Dwayne. *Have a nice life,* I thought.

And then the biggie: what about . . . Neil?

Whenever I asked, which I did every three or four seconds, the doctors would just look grave and the nurses tried to distract me with more forms to fill out. That scared the hell out of me . . . they don't try to confuse you like that unless they have something real bad they're trying not to have to tell you.

What I was most concerned about, after Neil's life, was whether they'd have to amputate his leg.

I was still worrying that one around when the lawyer poked his head in, followed by his Jaggaresque body. He was going bald, but didn't want anyone to know it, so he combed his hair long on one side and flopped it over. It really fooled you—for about half-a-second.

"Feeling a little better, Miss Taylor?" he asked.

I jumped. I thought he was talking to the voice in my head! Then I realized he just meant me, and I nodded.

"Good. Now get out of here, Mandy; I've got some stuff to discuss with Indiana Taylor here."

Mother Dearest clucked a few more times, fulfilling her job description, then departed. I didn't remember having met Martin Booth, esquire, before, but he sat down in the chair and started talking to me like we were old friends. "Come on, Jeanette, tell me the whole story. Everything . . . don't leave any juicy bit out, no matter how weird it sounds."

I opened my mouth, but he suddenly leaned forward and whispered, "And keep your voice *down;* if the police overhear, they might try to sneak it in if they ever decide to have a hearing or something."

"A h-hearing?" I'd known it was a possibility; but I didn't like to hear a lawyer mentioning it so casually.

"Jeanette, be reasonable. A kid is dead, and the cops are going to be interested in exactly what happened, don't you think? They might just take your word for it . . . I'll do everything I can to get that outcome. But I can't guarantee it. Maybe the police chief has the news goons sniffing after him and he gets on his high horse and decides to make an example. Or maybe he just bought a bad suit, and now he's down on tailors. But I have to warn you: a hearing is actually pretty likely. This town doesn't get much of this sort of thing."

I took a deep breath, held it, and let it out; then I started at the beginning and made a real production of it, stretching the story out a couple of hours. What the heck, it's not like I had somewhere to go that night.

I was freaked a little at first, pouring out my heart to like this total stranger; but he made all the right um-hm and hmm noises, and I settled down. He believed me, too—or at least he did a good job of psyching me out.

The way it works, anything you say to the attorney is covered under attorney-client privilege, which is the privilege to have your lawyer keep his big mouth shut. It doesn't matter what you say—he can't tell the cops, and they can't use it even if he did, which he wouldn't anyway.

In other words, even if I had murdered Bill Hicks in cold blood—which I didn't!—I could tell my attorney and ask what the hell to do about it.

He can't tell you to lie, but he *can* tell you to zip it and usually does.

In my case, though, Booth said we should talk to the police . . . with him sitting right at my elbow like Robert Shapiro next to O.J., whispering in my ear if he needs to tell me anything.

We decided that tomorrow would be a good day to do that. I was already starting to feel sick—I had

strep but didn't know it yet—and the doctors wanted
to keep me overnight for observation.

And then the night nurse, a chubby girl not a
whole lot older than I (I think she was actually a
candy-striper, not a real nurse) with dirty-blond hair
and a permanent frown, clumped in to ask what I
wanted to eat (everything and nothing: I was starving, but my throat was hurting like crazy). I asked
her about Neil, and she, Dolores, said, "Oh, I was
supposed to tell you. He's in surgery now."

Well, I nearly jumped right out of bed and ran to
see, but she wrestled me down. Dolores was quite a
bit stronger than she looked and used her weight to
good effect.

"Settle! Settle!" she barked, while Martin Booth
watched with amusement, grinning like a kid at the
circus.

"Why didn't anyone tell me he needed surgery? Is
he going to be all right? What's wrong? Is it his leg?
Is it going to have to come off? Will he be able to
walk again?"

She didn't or couldn't answer, insisting instead I
devote my full consciousness to picking out a menu.
I absently pointed at the paper sheet; served me
right—I ended up with broccoli and non-dairy
cheese casserole that was almost as good as airline
food.

I sat in the bed, knees drawn up and arms wrapped
around them, staring morosely at the opposite wall.
All I could think of was Neil dying on the table. Neil

ending up a cripple for the rest of his life. Neil vegging out under the anesthetic and never waking up, just lying there in a coma for the next fifty years. Booth wisely decided to cut and see me again in the morning.

I didn't sleep. Despite the pain, I had managed to wolf down the entire casserole. But my throat got progressively scratchier, and then the fever started. I knew I was thin; I'd lost some weight during the ordeal; but I didn't realize how much until Dolores walked me down the hall to a balance-scale. I was dressed in that stupid robe that doesn't quite close in the back, letting everyone see my butt.

They were probably disappointed if they did. I discovered I weighed *a hundred and five pounds,* which I hadn't weighed since I was thirteen years old! I felt truly weak, and no wonder. I'd lost about fifteen pounds in just a few days . . . probably mostly water-weight; we'd been chronically dehydrated.

I really felt sick when I returned to my bed, and it *finally* occurred to me that since I was in a hospital, I might as well tell someone. So I told Dolores. Before I could live to regret my indiscretion, I was surrounded by what seemed like a couple of hundred doctors (actually three), all poking me and making me strip (thanks) so they could check for spots or welts or something. I felt like a scarecrow, about as far from sexy as it was physically possible to be.

Finally they told me I had strep, and it would go away but I'd have a sore throat and a fever for a few days. Then they gave me two aspirin. I asked if I should call them in the morning, but none of them got it.

I was too sick even to ask about Dwayne and Samma; but I did insist they tell me about Neil. All I got was that he had survived the surgery, and anything else would depend on whether Neil Armstrong's parents were willing to waive their privacy rights. That sounded ominous; but at least I was glad to hear that both Neil's parents had shown up. Generally, since the divorce, they couldn't stand to be in the same room together.

I went to bed, and after tossing fitfully and sleeplessly for two or three seconds, dropped into the dreamless . . . and slept for two days!

All right, not continuously. Dolores or her little sidekick Bruce woke me up now and then to offer more food, which I devoured greedily—the doctors were worried about my weight, so they actually prescribed fattening food, hot damn!—and the vampires reappeared like clockwork to suck my blood and peer down my throat.

But mostly I slept. Booth reappeared to tell me the police had indefinitely postponed my interview, and my three living grandparents showed up to spell Mother Dearest, who couldn't take anymore time off work without being fired. I swear, she works for Ebenezer Scrooge!

Oh, but he was a tightfisted hand at the grindstone. Scrooge! a squeezing, wrenching, grasping, scraping, clutching, covetous old sinner! Hard and sharp as flint, from which no steel had ever struck out generous fire; secret, and self-contained, and solitary as an oyster.

Somewhere in that weird, gray period, I was visited by the helo pilot who rescued me. Dwayne was picked up by another guy, I found out.

I asked my pilot why there was only one person in his helicopter. "Wouldn't it make more sense to have a couple guys? Then I wouldn't have had to go crazy thinking the litter was going to flip over and dump Neil out."

He looked properly chagrined, but he had an excuse, it turned out. "I'm sorry, miss; I was already in the air, just searching, when I heard the radio call from the traffic newsguy. I just came to investigate; thought I could land and render medicals while you waited for real transport. But when I saw Mr. Armstrong just lying there like that, I suddenly decided to get him to the hospital immediately." His face had turned steadily redder; by the time he finished, he was actually mauve. "I guess I messed up; I'm really, really sorry."

"You didn't hose up," I said, "You probably saved his life. I'll never forget you—can you give me your name and address? I want to send you a card or some candy or something."

"Send it to the station," quoth he, still embarrassed

and grinning self-consciously. "We love getting stuff. Especially edible stuff." He gave me the address of Station 96, and I wrote it down in my memory note-book, where I also wrote a complete account of everything that happened while I still remembered all the details.

But still, no one would talk to me about Neil.

Then an extraordinary thing happened. Janine and Cuda Armstrong, Neil's parents, came to visit me in my small, private room. Mother Dearest, who is *très* cool at times, disappeared, dragging Grandma and Grandpa Riggles and Grandpa Taylor behind her.

Mrs. Armstrong sat at the foot of my bed, while Mr. Armstrong went to the window and looked out-side. I did my best not to puke—nothing to do with them, you understand; but the strep seemed to have slid down into my stomach, and I felt nauseated all the time.

"So," I said, nervously licking my lips, "no one's told me anything except that Neil s-sur-sur . . . sur-vived the operation. Is he . . . still all right?"

I was so scared, I almost fainted before they could even answer. I had suddenly gotten a terrible vision of complications setting in *after* the operation, and Neil . . . dying.

"He's alive and awake, honey," said Mrs. Arm-strong. I'd always liked her; but she seemed so reserved, I could never really think of her as a friend. She was always just Neil's mother, and maybe some-day my . . . oh, but that was silly. And premature.

I waited, not asking. She continued. "He asked us to come speak to you before you saw him. Jeanette, the break was bad, really bad. It was compound; that means . . . I don't want to go into it. Neil can tell you."

"I know what compound means. Did they—were they able to save the leg?" That was the biggie, now that I knew he was alive and conscious.

Janine Armstrong looked at her ex, but he was no help. He was staring out the window into the bright sunlight like he might find a wish somewhere under all the gold.

She looked back at me. "No, dear. They had to amputate. Just below the knee. I'm sorry."

Seventeen

I got that surreal feeling again, like I was floating above my own body, looking down and watching it react—but some *other* girl's body, not mine. Mrs. Armstrong's voice sounded like it came from the bottom of a well, and my flesh felt prickly all over, pins and needles, like when your foot falls asleep, but everywhere all at once.

"I . . . uh . . . guess . . ." I was stammering. I didn't know what to say, so of course I said something stupid and insensitive. "I guess he won't be going into the astronaut training program after all."

I had Cuda's attention at last. He turned toward me, totally surprised. "My son said he wanted to do that? Strange; he never told me."

I stared. I didn't know what to say. It was so sad . . . becoming an astronaut was Neil's greatest dream—and he hadn't even told his father, who *was* an astronaut, or had been when he was younger.

Maybe it was because Mr. Armstrong had never managed to make it onto a mission, even after eleven years in the program; there were cutbacks, and he was RIFfed out. Or maybe it was because Neil and Mr. Armstrong just didn't talk. Neil always bragged about his dad to me—but he never told any stories about how Dad did this or Dad did that, with his son, just what Dad did in the program.

"Huh, I never knew," said Mr. Armstrong, then turned back to the window, still dazed by the thought that his son had only a single leg now.

"Can I see Neil now, Mrs. Armstrong?"

"I wanted to prepare you for what it looks like. I don't want you flinching or getting sick in front of Neil, honey."

"I don't think I will, but prepare away."

She told me they'd had to cut it off because the break had punctured the flesh; and even with Samma's best bandage—it had saved his life, the doctor said—the wound got infected and gangrene set in. Another day, and Neil would have died anyway.

They'd cut the bone deeper than the surrounding flesh, so they could pull the muscle and skin together and suture them, leaving a rounded knob. Lots of stitches; pretty gory. I won't gag you.

Neil was in high spirits, but his mother thought he was faking it for her benefit. She wanted to dump me off with him, hoping I could snap him out of it so he could really come to terms with losing a leg.

Dolores appeared and refused to allow me to walk the entire thirty-foot marathon to Neil's room; she plopped me in a wheelchair and rolled me, "for insurance reasons," she said.

Neil wouldn't look at me when I first arrived. Dolores vanished, leaving me alone with my guy.

"Shoulda looked before you leaped, Leap," I said, half-laughing at my own joke.

"Feeble," said Neil.

"What did you expect? I've been sick."

"Hm."

I watched his face, my heart pounding a Stewart Copeland–style drum rhythm. I'd never seen anything so beautiful . . . how could I have looked at it before and just seen my buddy Neil, not a Greek god?

"Neil . . ." I leaned forward, put my hand on his head, "I know how much you wanted to join the program. But there're other ways into space; maybe by the time you're old enough, they'll be taking ordinary people like you and me."

He smiled; Mrs. Armstrong was right; he *was* faking it. I can tell. "Oh, I'm not worried about that, Jet Stream." Liar! "I'm sure after a while, I won't even miss the leg." Liar! "I'm just worried that from now on, people will treat me differently."

"Anyone in particular?"

"Huh? Oh no, no one in particular." Liar, liar! "Just

people in general might start to treat me like a crip-....a disabled person."

I leaned close to whisper in his ear, "Don't be stupid, Neil! I said we were an item, and I won't change my mind just because you're one foot shorter."

"What? I'm not any shorter . . . oh, I see what you mean. One foot, ho ho." He put his head back, and for the first time since I entered his room, seemed honestly relieved. "Are we an item? I don't remember you saying anything like that—h-honey."

"I don't mean I said it to you! I said it to myself, and that's the important thing. And don't call me honey; it makes us sound like we've been married for seven years. Call me dearest, or dear heart, or better yet, just Jet Stream. I'm kind of used to it, Leap."

He opened his eyes and turned to me. "Jet, what about Samma?"

"Oh, she's all right with it. She's set her sights on Dwayne the boyjock."

"No, dearest . . . *what about Samma?*"

"Yeah. Well, I don't mind if you stay friends with her. So long as it's behind my back." I clenched my teeth so hard, my jaw ached; my tongue once again worried the missing half a tooth. "I don't want to know about it. I don't know any Samma Glynnis . . . she's dead to me."

"You OK with that?"

"I told you my standards, Neil. She was the only one of you who turned her back on me. Don't ever mention her again in my presence, kiddo, if you know what's good for you."

I was trying to be light; but he saw right through me. He knew I was dead serious. Neil nodded, and we moved onto another subject.

"So how serious an item are we, Jet?"

"Serious enough. You can go public with it. But I don't have any plans to get married or anything, not until after college and graduate school. Let's just commit to a few months right now, till we see how it's going."

"The police interviewed me about you. Did Mom tell you?"

"No! She didn't say a thing," I lied. When he finally got around to showing me his leg, I didn't want him to know I'd been coached.

"Yeah . . . I thought about saying I'd seen the whole thing; but then I figured they'd already talked to Dwayne, since he wasn't injured, and probably she-who-shall-remain-nameless, and I'd better not try to get cute. I told them the truth: I wasn't there and didn't see a thing."

"Yeah; unfortunately, neither did Dwayne. It's my word against a dead man's . . . and Dwayne is probably so uncool, he told them about Bill having attacked me. So they know I had a motive."

I hadn't realized until that moment just how scared I was. I didn't want to go to prison—not when all I'd done was defend myself! But how could I prove I was telling the truth?

"Oh," said Neil suddenly, "happy birthday, bear-heart!"

"That's *dear*-heart, you clod! Not bear-heart . . . hey, what do you mean, happy birthday?" I stared at my watch, and damned if he wasn't right! It *was* my birthday . . . and I hadn't even realized it in all the excitement.

Happy seventeen, Jeanette; even Miss Taylor was joining the party.

"I think the hospital is going to give you a cake later."

"Cool."

"You need fattening up. See? You *can* be too thin."

"But not too rich."

Abruptly, Neil fell back, wincing. "Ah . . . Jet? I think . . . I think I better get some rest now. Like. I mean, I'm still on the painkillers."

I gently stroked his hair. "You sleep now, kiddo. I'll still be here." I climbed up onto the bed next to my beloved. "Enjoy this while it lasts, Leap; this'll be the last time we go to bed together for a long time." But Neil was already asleep and missed the joke.

I lay on my stomach, feeling Neil's chest expand and contract with every breath. If they wanted me for a birthday celebration, they'd have to catch me first. I drifted into a doze.

Dolores shook me awake a couple of minutes later. Turned out to be an hour-and-a-half. "Mr. Armstrong's mother is just outside."

"Neil's grandmother? Oh—you mean his mother."

"I figured you didn't want her to see you like this."

"Probably not wise." I pulled myself painfully to my feet and sat down in the wheelchair again, still half-asleep.

"Besides, they want you back in your own room. It's a surprise."

"Oh, the cake," I said, totally forgetting my manners in my still-waking-up daze.

"Somebody's been shooting off his mouth," sniffed Dolores, glaring at Neil's sleeping form.

Back in my room, the candy-striper brought in a cake with eighteen unlit candles..."one to grow on," I guess, though I didn't particularly want to do any more growing.

"Hand me my backpack," I said. I rummaged and found the film canister with the last three matches, the ones I'd never had to use once I figured out how to make fire the old-fashioned way.

I struck the first match—then again, then again. I couldn't get it to light.

The second match broke, but again, it remained stubbornly unlit.

The third match was as useless as the other two. I laughed like a loon . . . good thing I *hadn't* relied on them! I'd have starved and frozen to death!

In the middle of the party, if you can call it that— Mother Dearest appeared with Jaq in tow, but my little brother seemed totally bored by the whole adventure—Booth stuck his head inside. "Can I talk to the birthday girl?" he asked. "I've got a wonderful present for her, but it's private."

He steered me into the chair and wheeled me slowly through the corridor. "The police have closed the file, Jeanette. They're not going to prosecute."

I stared, stunned to silence.

"They believe you."

"But . . . but why? I haven't even talked to them yet."

"I told them your story. I was right; they were very skeptical. Frankly, I don't think they believed you could have kicked Hicks off the cliff, even in self-defense. They thought you had cut the rope and let him fall . . . didn't say it directly, but I got a sense."

"So what—what changed their minds? Not that I'm complaining, mind you."

Booth smiled impishly. "They got statements from Neil, Samma, and Dwayne, but none of them helped you because none of them was present. But they finally got an eyewitness account who corroborated your story."

"What? Who?" I was like totally confused.

"Bill Hicks."

I stared. This was too bizarro for words. "Bill? An eyewitness?"

"Jeanette, they found his body. It had only been washed about five miles downriver. And you know what he had, Jeanette?"

"What?"

"Your knife . . . still tucked neatly into his belt. Bill had the knife, Jeanette—and that proves your story beyond a reasonable doubt, and even the cops believe you now."

I chuckled. Then I started to laugh. I guess the other patients must've thought I was part hyena, the way I howled. It wasn't humor; it was more of a release . . . days and days of being absolutely convinced I was going to fry for a self-defense killing that was not just legal, it was righteous. I would spend eternity in a little room in Hell with Bill Hicks, me, and a paper knife.

"So . . . that's it?"

"That's all she wrote, Jeanette. The fat lady sang, and the DA has definitely decided not to file. Their own coroner has listed the death as natural causes; they're not even going to go public with the self-defense thing, and I advise you not to, either."

"Go public? What do you mean, call a press conference?"

"You don't have to, Miss Taylor; the press has already called one. You're going to get the full treatment because of the medal."

"The *what?*"

Booth grinned like a rube at the circus. "You don't know, do you? Jeanette, the whole nation has been following your ordeal for more than a week now."

"They . . . have?"

"And your story has made top story on the four

networks for three days straight now. You've had your fifteen minutes of fame, and you're not done yet. The people are just lapping it up off the plate . . . it's such a change from all the negative crap they see all the time. The President—"

"The *President?*" This was getting surreal!

"Of the United States has awarded you the Medal of Freedom, the highest one you can get without being in uniform. The ceremony is a week from Thursday. You'll get to meet Bill Clinton, girl."

"Jesus. Just . . . *Jesus!*" I don't care what your politics are . . . it's just totally, way cool to meet the actual President of the United States—even if I wasn't quite old enough to vote yet.

"And as if that wasn't enough, the San Glendora City Council is also going to give you an award for bravery."

"The City Council? *Bravery?* That's like getting a medal for chastity awarded by Ted Kennedy."

Bravery? I didn't even know what that meant anymore. I didn't do anything out of bravery; I was scared all the time, and I never had a choice!

Well . . . but I *did* have a choice: I could have given in to terror; I could have let Bill rape me or throw me off the cliff; I could have just given up instead of climbing that layback after Bill died; I could have just dropped into the water, or let Samma drown.

I guess courage is when you just keep going, even

when you're scared and exhausted to death, and do what you have to do.

"It was that throwing-stick brainstorm that did it, Jeanette; Dwayne Cors told us all about it. And I warn you in advance . . . all the newsies are going to ask about Bill. As your attorney, I recommend you show them just how sorry and sad you are that he fell into the water like that. If they ask about you kicking him, just look confused and let me answer it."

"But I'm not! I had to do it; it was him or me."

"I said *show them* you're sorry; I didn't ask how you *really* felt. Besides, you're sorry the whole thing happened, aren't you?"

"Well . . . yeah, I guess." The strange thing was—I really wasn't. Don't get me wrong; I didn't want to be attacked and have to kill my used-to-be best friend! But it's an amazing thing to know that you really, truly can take care of yourself.

For that knowledge, I'd put up with an awful lot. You know, the whole Nietzsche thing.

I lay back in the chair while he rolled me up onto the roof. It was a beautiful, bright, hot night, and nearly all my questions in life had been answered. All but one.

"Did the cops check up on Lalla? I told you to ask them about her."

"They checked. They're not sure of what they found. A girl did go missing out of Austin, Texas a few weeks before Bill left: a sixteen-year-old named Leslie Lana Brutin disappeared a month and a half ago. The local authorities thought she was just a runaway; but she attended the same special-ed school that Bill attended, and several people said they were going out together."

"Was Leslie Lana ever called Lalla?"

"No, no one can remember calling her that."

"Well, maybe it was just Bill's nickname for her."

"Or maybe it was a different person altogether. They don't know, but it's close enough that they'll probably open an investigation."

"Well, that's it, then. That's all I have. Anything else?"

"Not so far as I know. I'll take you back to your room—happy birthday, Jeanette."

Late that night—about three in the morning, actually—I awoke, scared to death in my hospital bed. I couldn't remember where I was or why I was there.

Shaking, I got out of bed and padded down the corridor to Neil's room. I sat in the chair and watched him sleep; then he must have felt something, for he woke up and watched me back.

"Jet," he suddenly said out of the blue.

I jumped, jerked away from a fitful, unpleasant half-dream. "You're awake?"

"Jet, I have a request."

"Yes?"

"When I get out of here…"

"Yesssss?"

"You've got to promise one thing: that you'll never call me peg-leg."

248 Dafydd ab Hugh

I laughed again. But this time it was a regular laugh, not that cackling, lunatic laugh with which I'd scared old Martin Booth. Then my tongue found the missing tooth, as it had been doing every few minutes for days on end now.

"So long as you don't call *me* Alfred E. Newman, kiddo. Deal?"

Neil spat into his hand; I spat into mine, and we shook. It was the next best thing to a formal engagement.

The adventure continues in

SWEPT AWAY:
THE PIT

Coming from HarperPaperbacks in
June 1996

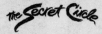

BABY-SITTER'S NIGHTMARES
Terror Beyond Your Wildest Dreams

ALONE IN THE DARK By Daniel Parker

A huge mansion on the beach, a fancy sportscar, a hot tub—and a kid who knows everything about Gretchen . . . including her deadly future!

A KILLER IN THE HOUSE By J. H. Carroll

Sue knows she shouldn't be sneaking around the Anderson's property after little Adam goes to bed. But baby-sitting can be so boring. Then Sue stumbles upon a strange envelope. An envelope with a mystery inside—a deadly mystery. Will Sue survive the night?

LIGHTS OUT By Bernard O'Keane

Something is coming for Moira. Something hungry. Something evil. Something that can't be stopped . . .

THE EVIL CHILD By M. C. Sumner

William is different from the other kids Toni's had to baby-sit for. He's smart—too smart. And he can build things—deadly things. And if Toni isn't careful, William may test his wicked inventions on her.

WHEN THE MOON IS IN THE SEVENTH HOUSE . . .
BEWARE

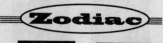

#1 STAGE FRIGHT (LEO)
Lydia loves the spotlight, but the stage she is on is set for danger.

#2 DESPERATELY YOURS (VIRGO)
Someone at Fairview High will do anything for attention, and they may give Virginia a *killer* deadline.

#3 INTO THE LIGHT (LIBRA)
The line is blurry between Lydia's reality and her fantasy-world mural. What happens when her mural is slated for destruction?

#4 DEATH GRIP (SCORPIO)
Sabrina wants to avenge her boyfriend's death, which she knows was no accident—but revenge can be costly.